JOTUNHEIMS QUEEN

Frozen Hearts Book One

Lucinda Greyhaven

Copyright © 2022 by Lucinda Greyhaven

All rights reserved. No part of this book may be used or reproduced in any form whatsoever without written permission except in the case of brief quotations in critical articles or reviews.

This book is a work of fiction. Names, characters, businesses, organizations, places, events and incidents either are the product of the author's imagination or are used fictitiously. Any resemblance to actual persons, living or dead, events, or locales is entirely coincidental.

Poems Copyright Edgar Allan Poe

Printed in the United States of America.

Cover design by Getcovers.com

Second Edition: April 2023

CONTENTS

JOTUNHEIMS QUEEN I

Prologue
Chapter One: The God of Being Naughty
Chapter Two: Ice Realms and Dreamscapes
Chapter Three: Apprentice Witchling
Chapter Four: Odin Oath Breaker
Chapter Five: One Last Visitation
Chapter Six: The Hospital Years
Chapter Seven: Without Her
Chapter Eight: Rediscovery on Midgard
Chapter Nine: Therapy
Chapter Ten: Loki Returns to Midgard
Chapter Eleven: Reunited
Chapter Twelve: Regrets
Chapter Thirteen: A Tower Moment
Chapter Fourteen: Loki's Choice
Chapter Fifteen: Trapped in the Castle
Chapter Sixteen: Escape and Tolerance
Chapter Seventeen: Grudging Cohabitation
Chapter Eighteen: Weapons Training
Chapter Nineteen: Loki's Shock

Chapter Twenty: Loki's Fury
Chapter Twenty-One: Frigg's Visitation
Chapter Twenty-Two: Odin's Warning
Chapter Twenty-Three: A Secret Ability
Chapter Twenty-Four: Something There That....
(Or Loki Finally Admits His Feelings)
Chapter Twenty-Five: Wasn't There Before
Chapter Twenty-Six: Loki's Sacrifice

ABOUT THE AUTHOR **169**

Trigger warnings: sexual content, abuse, mental health, mental hospital ward, alcohol addiction.

Prologue

I stood on the icy cliff face, a white fur cloak shielding me from the raging storm as I prepared myself for the battle. I could feel the dagger at my waist, a weight that was still unusual to me. I pulled the fur lined gloves from my cold fingers ready to cast my spells as soon as he gave me the signal. I was ready to fight for my newfound people, giving my life for them if required. This fight was for him as much as it was for the army I was about to summon.

I had to force myself not to laugh at the sheer insanity of my life. Just under a year ago, I had been the messed up server on the fuck early shift, dreaming and begging the universe for something more. Something that I could feel a part of, where I wasn't so eternally alone. Now, I was engaged to the God of Mischief and about to wage war in the eternal realm. I was fighting for our lives and the lives of every single human on Midgard, as well as every living being on Jotunheim.

All those crazy ass conspiracy theorists saying that the next world war would be in the astral realm, constantly posting all over social media about the events that were coming. All those insane comments that Hitler had been training his army with black magic to make them more powerful, ready to destroy anything that came after him. I had thought that my father was off his rocker when he had told me in my teens; that he had seen one too many late night tv shows. He had always believed in aliens, monsters, ufos and all kinds of strange things that normal people thought were pure fantasy. I am confident that the school board would have taken me away if they had seen what he was educating me with.

Now I wished that I had paid more attention to his crazy ranting, it might have helped me understand my current situation a little better. As well as listened harder to, or written down the oral tales of the Norse Pantheon that my grandmother used to tell me whenever she was around. I might have had an easier time accepting what I was living with. I continuously felt like I was going insane, that I would wake up tomorrow back in the padded cell of my childhood.

Then I saw him, those stunning green eyes looking over at me with a mixture of adoration, love, and concern. I smiled back, nodding acceptance. This was my time to shine. My chance to prove to all the haters, the fake God Spouses and trolls why I and I alone, was Loki's Queen. I would not let my husband down, not today. I started to draw my power, closing my eyes, losing myself to the sensations flowing through me. Loki would have his army.

Jotunheims Queen

Chapter One

The God of Being Naughty

A small blonde girl running around in a back garden in the rain, shouting happily. Chanting for a storm. An older woman came out to her, her grandmother. "Holly, what are you doing sweetheart? You will get soaked."

"I want a storm, not just silly rain."

"Well, you will have to ask Thor a little more nicely if you want that. Not just shout at him."

"Who is Thor, Grandma?"

"Thor is the Norse God of Thunder. He makes the lightning come from a giant hammer he carries."

"Cool! Can I have a giant hammer too?"

"Maybe when you are older. Now come out the rain and warm up and I will tell you all about Thor, and perhaps some of the other old Gods as well."

● ●

Thor looked down fondly on the Midgardian scene, "I like this one, she is clever."

Loki looked down at the image in the pool as well, as he sharpened his daggers. "Then she does not suit you at all, 'brother.' "

Thor rolled his eyes at the heckling about his intelligence. "Be a little kinder Loki, she would greatly benefit from your teachings as well. She could learn much from someone as wise and talented as you."

Loki laughed bitterly, sheaving the current dagger, before pulling out the next. "No Thor, I would only corrupt the innocent. Besides, I would not take one of your followers. That woman has even given her a small hammer to wear for protection. It is better that you remain her patron."

"Your loss Loki, is my gain as always."

"Don't singe her hair when you teach her how to channel lightning," he retorted.

"I will get her to singe your tangled locks if you don't brush them soon."

"Don't threaten me Mr of Thunder or I will show her how to set your whole body on fire."

••

A middle-aged woman stood screaming at the blonde child. "You are a bad, evil, wicked, devil spawn of a child. How dare you refuse to clean your room as I told you to! I do not care that you are faking being sick, you will do as you are told, or you will be punished!"

"I am not faking. I am sick, just like Daddy is."

"No, your father is ill, he needs to be kept warm. You are just attention seeking. Up to your room right now and don't you dare come back down until dinner!" she screeched.

"But it's so cold up there, and I need the bathroom," the girl objected, trying to move around her mother to get to the bathroom.

Her mother blocked the end of the stairs to prevent her coming down. "I said up to your room right now! I'll get you your potty."

The girl looked at her in horror. "I am far too old for a potty. I am going to the bathroom!"

The woman hit the child hard around the face. "Last warning, get to your room right now, before I tan your hide so hard that you can't sit down for a month. And no books! You are not allowed to read any of your books for at least a week or until you deserve to have them back again. You are an evil, disgusting, attention-seeking bitch!"

Days passed by with the girl alone in her room, upset and alone. When she was finally allowed back down into the garden, she sat on the grass reading a book quietly, alone, not bothering anyone. The mother walks by with a basket of washing. "I told you about not reading for at least a week, you wicked deceitful monster!" She snatched the book so hard that pages came loose.

*"No, you said that I couldn't read any of **my** books, this is not one of my books. This book belongs to daddy, I got it from his shelf. So, I didn't break your stupid rules," the child objected.*

Smack

Right around the little girl's face. It hurt so much she blinked back tears, yet still somehow stayed defiantly staring back at her mother, the look of hurt and betrayal clear.

"Right little Lady Loki, aren't you? Think you are so very clever. So clever that you will cut yourself one day. Fine, if you want it so much, keep the book." She threw it at the child. "This is the last book you will see in an extremely long time; I hope it was worth it. Now, get to your room before I change my mind, and don't let me see you outside of it before morning!"

Crying, the girl picked up the book, trying to repair the loose pages before running back to her room that was more like a prison cell.

The next day, the parents went out leaving the child in the care of her grandmother. They were picnicking in the garden; the child had a pile of brand-new books next to her. "Grandma, who is Loki?"

"Why do you want to know that?" she asked, bringing a tray of drinks over.

"Mummy said I was being a 'lady Loki' because I said I was reading Daddy's book, so I did not deserve to be punished. She said I could not read any of my books. Not that I couldn't read any book."

"Did you? Well, that was a very clever thing to work out. Loki is the Norse God of Mischief and like a blood brother to Thor," she answered.

The mother returned to the house, glaring through the window at the cute little picnic scene. "Tell the monster the truth about her idol. He is also the God of lies, wickedness and deception. He gets people killed and hurts good people for no reason."

The child ignored her. "What is mischief?"

"Well, kind of like playing tricks and things. Like he cut Sif's hair while she was sleeping. Sif is Thor's wife."

"So, a God of being naughty?" the child asked.

"Kind of, yes."

"Yay! I want to follow a God of being naughty. I love Loki even more than I love Thor! Loki is so cool!"

"Oh, you would, wouldn't you? An evil little thing like you would want to follow an evil God. Like breeds like always. You want an informative book to read, get out your bible. Learn why it is wrong to worship any other so-called Gods. And you, stop filling the things head with such utter nonsense," the mother demanded.

"I'll fill her head with whatever I like, she needs someone to take care of her."

••

Thor was looking down at his smallest worshipper again through the pool. "Loki, come here." He heard a huff as the red-haired man came over to him.

"What do you want oaf?" Loki demanded, he was suffering from a hangover and in no mood for any stupidity.

"That girl, she is chanting your name as well now brother. Can't you hear her prayer?"

"And why would she do that? She is your little pet mage not mine."

"She was told that you are the God of being Naughty."

Loki sighed heavily, feeling several thousand years older at that comment. Heavily considering grabbing a bottle of mead for a little hair of the dog to fix his pounding head. "All these thousands of years, all I have created, all that I have done and what am I to be remembered for? The God of being naughty. I need a drink, or fifty. Midgardians! I swear I do not understand your blind fascination!"

"You would with this one, she shows cunning, skill, intelligence. I can teach her a little, but brother, she would thrive under your tutoring. Could you not bring yourself to aid someone so small?" Thor pleaded.

Loki looked down on her, "Perhaps, but she is one of yours. I do not take another God's property. I am already demonised enough, do you not think?" He sighed again. "God of being naughty," he muttered, "By the Norns."

"Loki, please, she is a child. She means no disrespect. She is just trying to understand something much bigger than she is. Please, show a mortal some mercy."

"Thor, go and teach your pet mortal and leave me alone. I have better things to do with my time." Loki stormed off to find something to dull the aching in his head.

Thor looked down again on the child. "Give him time my dear, he will come around. You will make him. It is long since time that he remembered you again."

Jotunheims Queen

Chapter Two

Ice Realms and Dreamscapes

Loki pulled his coat closer around his frame as he walked through, or more like waded through the deep snow. He did not feel the cold, it was more the emotional warmth he missed from always being alone these dark centuries. Yes, he had spouses, children and even the odd friend after a fashion. Meer dalliances to distract him from the gaping wound of loneliness in his soul. No one wanted to be too close to Loki, he was demonised even now. Eons after the first Ragnarök had come and gone, and many more besides. He was still seen as a traitor and Odin as the all powerful All Father instead of Odin Oath breaker, as he was to Loki. Those who insisted that Odin was the all father, not the some father had never been on his darker side. If only it could be seen that Loki had done what he had done at Ragnarök to prevent something far worse from happening. Ragnarök had to happen, Odin had to die to be reborn in the new era thereafter. Refreshed in his magic and purpose to move on to greater things.

Even the history books only remembered Loki as a drunken womanising creature that played tricks and ruined everyone's lives. The victors wrote the history. His tactical mind, the planning he put into their battles, the times he had saved their asses all forgotten about. Even his genderfluid, shapeshifting, pansexual nature was completely deleted from record. Homophobia was certainly not a modern invention.

As he stomped through the cold, Loki thought to himself about Thor's little apprentice. He had been far too hard on her; she was just a child. And children related complex matters in ways they could understand. Just like his own children had done over the years. He would take a moment to slip down to Midgard and see her. Drop a few hints on how to improve her skills. The parents seemed toxic enough to require an intervention from a deity and Thor had given permission to attend. He could find the time to have a little fun with that mother figure. It had been long since he had felt like pranking anyone.

Loki was brought sharply from his thoughts by the sound of a child laughing. This was Jotunheim, the depths of the wilderness. No one ever came here, which is why he had made himself a home here in the cave systems where no one would find him. How could a child be out here? He could not remember when the last Jotun child had been born. There were few of them left after the wars and Ragnarök's. Living so deep in the caverns they almost never came to the surface.

He turned a corner by the mountain and saw what looked like a Midgardian child building a snowman of all things. A young girl, ten at most, dressed in a thin night dress and socks that were both soaked through. The girl looked a little familiar, wasn't this Thor's apprentice? How was she here and why?

As she threw a snowball at the snowman it shattered hitting the edge of Loki's coat. "Uh oh," she muttered as she turned around. "Sorry Mr, I didn't think anyone was here. There never usually is."

Loki painstakingly erased the look of disgust on his face from the slowly melting snow covering his best coat and tried to smile at her. "That is all right little one, I was thinking the same thing. I have never seen another person here."

She looked at him. "Do you live here Mr?"

Loki nodded. "I have for a long time now."

The girl looked sad. "Does that mean I can't play here anymore?"

The look on her face broke his ice filled heart, how could he refuse her? "No little one, I have no objection to sharing my home with you. You may play here as often as you wish. However, I do insist that you dress more warmly when you come here so you do not fall ill. I will not nurse you if you should." He took his long coat off, wrapping it around her. "Take this for now, while I build a fire." It crossed his mind that she was not just an astral projecting 'ghost,' she could touch, and feel. Was she building her own body when she got here or was she shifting her entire self in her sleep? Either way, she was much more powerful than her age should allow.

"Won't you be cold?" she asked, looking at the thin tunic he wore. She held the hem out to him. "We could share?"

What a sweetheart. Loki could not help but smile back at the child. "That is very nice of you, but I do not feel the cold that much." Loki started to clear the snow, building up rocks to make a fire pit.

The girl, satisfied, wrapped the coat tighter around herself to watch him. "What's your name? I can't keep calling you Mr."

Loki paused in the middle of taking some firewood from his pack, it did not seem timely to reveal who he was. He did not want to scare her, what Midgardian name would be suitable? "Luke," he decided. "My name is Luke, and what is yours little one? Or shall I just call you the Snow Princess?"

She rolled her eyes. "Holly. My dad wanted me to be his Holly Hobby doll forever and ever, but my mother says I am as prickly and nasty as the bush."

"Your mother sounds quite the unpleasant person to be around," he commented as he continued to build the fire. "I shall call you Ase, in my language it means goddess."

"I'm not a goddess, I am not even wanted. My mother keeps telling me that I am wicked and evil," she said sadly. "That's why I come here, people leave me alone here."

"Ase, you have managed to travel here all by yourself. That is no easy feat even for an advanced mage and you are untrained in magic. There is more to you than you currently think."

"My mother says magic is not real."

Loki's eyes sparkled as he smiled at her. "Oh, is it not?" He flexed his fingers towards the sticks he had lain. Blue fire sprung from the wood, flames reaching up to warm them both.

"Wow!" Holly exclaimed, coming closer to warm her cold hands. "That is so awesome!"

"Thank you Ase." He was choked up, no one had ever in his lifetime thought that his magic was interesting or exciting.

"But why is it blue?"

Loki sat on the snow next to the child. "Because my body creates blue fire. Would you like to see?"

"Yeah!"

"Do not touch me, as you may be harmed," he warned. He closed his eyes, calling the fire, feeling it flicker across his arms and chest.

"Wow!" she exclaimed again. "That is so pretty! You make pretty fire! Not boring red fire."

Loki chuckled to himself. "Now, that is not a common reaction to my magic Ase."

"Well, anyone who thinks it is not cool is a stupid, silly person. Because it is! I wish I could do that too!"

"Perhaps you will be able to one day." Loki pulled the fire back into himself.

She reached out to touch his now cool, normal looking skin as her mind tried to process what it had seen. Loki pulled back the sleeve of his tunic letting her explore to see he was not burned. "Why do you have scars?" she asked.

Loki cursed himself for momentarily forgetting that there was a reason he never showed his arms. "From battle, a long time ago." He pulled his arm back covering them.

"Battle scars do not look like that."

Loki's heart sank that a child could understand something so dark. "Do you have scars like that Ase?"

She pulled her sleeve up to show several on her upper arm, some old, some still oozing.

"Oh Ase." Loki sighed, running his thumb over the wounds healing them. "I truly regret that you know any of this."

Holly shrugged. "That's life." She looked away, as if she heard something. "I'm sorry Mr, I have to go."

She vanished before he could answer, leaving him alone with the fire and his dark thoughts. His realm seemed just that little bit lesser for her departure. Loki turned back towards his cave to try and get some rest, but his mind was full of a little girl who needed a real friend.

Lucinda Greyhaven

Chapter Three

Apprentice Witchling

Time passed without Loki seeing his new little friend that much, he thought little of it. She would be back if she wanted to be, he was not exactly popular when people were looking for company. He found her playing in the snow a few times, keeping his distance so as not to disturb her. Before he had her made a suit of warm winter clothing in his signature green. Boots, coat with a fur hood, leather skirt and bodice simple enough her small fingers would be able to put it on with ease. Leaving the package wrapped and protected by magic for when she visited again. He found himself leaving food and gifts in the hollow of an ice tree by the firepit. Books on magic, spelled so she would be able to read them in her own Midgardian tongue. The gifts always disappeared, a few mortal flowers, or a bracelet weaved by child hands left in their place. Now and then, even the odd Midgardian candy.

It must have been two years or more before they spoke again. Loki was bringing back a bag of supplies from another realm when he saw the green clad girl trying to build a fire the way he did, with magic. Her grunts of frustration as she could barely create sparks from her fingertips, looking more like sparklers than true flame. "Luke can do it, so I can do it too!" she muttered to herself.

Loki stood staring at her, trying to hold back his laughter. "Oh Ase, you can't spell cast until you learn your groundwork. Did those books teach you nothing?"

Holly jumped at his voice. "I tried the books, but I couldn't understand the words."

Loki picked up the book she had open on her knee and skimmed the beginner warding's chapters. "Perhaps this is a little too advanced for your age."

Holly pouted. "Does that mean I can't learn magic until I am older?"

"No Ase, it means I made a mistake in the books I gave you. It is not your fault at all. At your age, I was reading advanced books on magic, however I had been learning magic since I could walk and talk. I should have taken note that you were a complete beginner. My regrets," Loki answered. "If you care to come with me to my home, I can set up some wards and teach you myself. If you would like that?"

"Oh please, yes please. I want to learn!" Holly begged.

"Come Ase, I will make us dinner."

Loki took her with him to the cave, reaching his hand out to light the fire under the cauldron and the candles as they entered. Pulling off his damp coat to hang it on a jutting out rock, before helping Holly with her own coat and hanging it up.

Holly moved over to the fire warming herself. "Is this a spell?" she asked, looking into the cauldron.

"It's stew, venison stew. If you are going to practise magic in my realm, you need to eat in it as well. Or you will end up draining your magic to the point you start burning your life force instead. Do that too often and you will die."

"That's why you leave me snacks?"

"Yes, Ase. You must remember to eat here and eat well." Loki started pulling the furs from the floor, pushing the furniture back to create a space. He handed a bag of salt to the child. "Draw a circle and then stand in it."

"I saw this in movies, surely it isn't real?" she asked.

"Ase, do as you are told, or I will not teach you." Loki warned.

"Sorry Luke." Holly poured the salt to create a circle before climbing in it.

"Salt, chalk, iron and silver is protective. The cheapest bag of salt and you can make a safe space to cast in. Later I will teach you sigils and show you how to add candles, but for now. This will work fine," Loki promised. He sat cross legged on the floor outside the circle, indicating that she should do the same inside of it. "Close your eyes."

"I don't like the dark," Holly said quietly.

"Nor do I," Loki confessed quietly. He felt Holly reach out from the circle to squeeze his hand reassuringly. He took it, using his magic to enlarge the circle to include them both. "Ase, you need to focus on my voice, the crackling of the fire, the flickering of the candle flames. Listen to my words, I need you to picture a brick. A strong brick, made of any substance you like. See it, feel its texture under your fingertips, make it real to you in your mind. Once you can feel that brick, I need you to make another, and another. Build a wall with the bricks, and then make the wall into a house. Take as much time as you need. Focus on the building, think of it like the building blocks from your realm. Make it as real to you as my hand holding yours."

They sat there in silence as Holly did as she was bid. "What do I do now?" she asked.

"Now you have a house, build it a roof, a door, and then windows. Make a path towards it, a garden if you like. And then protect the house with whatever makes you feel safe. Broken glass, barbed wire, guns, weapons, creatures. Make it a safe place for you."

Another long pause as Holly did as she was bid. "I have cats, lots of cats."

Loki smiled. "Not fluffy pet ones I hope."

"Oh, they are, but they can grow into panthers, lions, tigers and scary cats." She smiled.

"Well done, Ase, next I want you to picture a key in your hand. The key to the front door. Decorate it as you will but make it original to yourself. Do not tell me how it looks, it must be your secret. When you are ready, use it to open the door and walk inside. Tell me what you see inside the house."

Holly moved her free hand as if she were unlocking a doorway. "I see a kitchen, with a fire and cats on the hearth. And doors leading off it, one to a long corridor full of doors, one to a sleeping area, with a bed and a wardrobe and one to a bathroom."

"Very good Ase. That long corridor is an entranceway to the realms, including here. The places between the realms can be dangerous. You should enter the house and walk down that corridor to open a door to where you need to go for safety. Otherwise, terrible things could follow you. When you sleep, go into the house and the bed and sleep there. It will protect you and your mind from harm."

"I understand."

Loki opened his eyes and released her hand. "You have done well Ase, it takes a great deal of skill to do what you have just done. Some master mages have still not created a home as effortlessly as you have."

"Can I open my eyes yet?" she asked, yawning.

"Yes Ase, open them and eat please." He started to serve them a meal from the cauldron.

Holly stood, swaying and almost fell into her guide. "Sorry," she mumbled.

"Ase, sit, rest," he admonished, giving her a bowl of the stew. She barely got to the end of it before she fell asleep leaning against him. Loki covered her with a blanket. "Ase, what are you doing to me? I shouldn't be stealing another God's apprentice." He looked at her sleeping so peacefully. "Do you know that no one has done this since my children were born?" he asked quietly. "You, young Ase, are going to melt this cold, icy heart if I don't stop you."

Jotunheims Queen

Chapter Four

Odin Oath breaker

Over the years that followed, Loki and Holly fell into a routine. Whenever she visited, Loki would set her some basic lessons. Teaching her how to find her 'centre' for her magic, how to protect herself and create wards. Even a little sword fighting and sleight of hand. No spells however, no real magic other than healing and how to create a fire. He was not sure how he felt about seeing his Ase on the battlefield casting powerful spells. Or how he felt about her risking getting hurt. Holly seemed happy enough in her lessons, chattering away. He had had to replace her winter clothing more times than he could count as she slowly grew up.

One night Loki would never forget was the night he had found her crying, hiding from him. The snow around her smeared with blood. "Ase, are you hurt? What has happened?" he demanded, calling on his magic to heal her.

"Nothing, leave me alone!"

"Ase, tell me where you are hurt, please?"

"Just go away!" she cried, pushing him away. She looked embarrassed.

"Oh." Loki realised what was wrong. "Are you bleeding from your womanly areas?"

"Shut up!" she snapped.

Loki sighed. "I think we need to have a little talk. Has your mother said nothing about womanly bleedings?"

"No! I do not want to die! Please, don't let me die!" she sobbed.

Loki pulled her into his arms. "Okay, firstly we are going to the hot springs so you can bathe. Secondly, we are going to have a nice friendly talk over some chamomile tea." He pulled her into his arms and carried her to the spring, deep in the caves where he lived. "Bathe, there are soaps and oils, take what are to your liking. I will bring you towels and fresh garments."

"I ruined the ones you gave me, I'm sorry. Please don't hate me," Holly begged.

"Ase, it is a little blood, it will wash out. There is no harm done, just go bathe, the warm water will ease the ache that is no doubt deep in your stomach."

Holly stripped to her underwear and climbed into the pool, washing as he had bid.

Loki used his magic to set up a curtain between them so he could not see her undressed, leaving clean clothing, bandages, towels, and tea for her. "Holly, when a woman becomes a woman, they grow the ability to create life inside of them. A baby."

"I know that my auntie is pregnant, but what has that got to do with me bleeding to death?"

Loki chuckled. "You won't die of these bleedings. Once a month, your body creates a lining and eggs so that you can carry a baby if a man puts the spark of life inside you, but how he does that is not a conversation I am willing to have with you currently. Without that spark of life, the lining and the egg rot and then you must bleed them out. It is normal and natural and will stop only when you reach an age where you can no longer carry a child, or you are with child."

"I have to go through this every single month?" Holly asked, her voice breaking from emotion.

"I regret to say yes, and for three to six days every month."

"How do I stop my clothes getting ruined?"

"I left you some bandages, you put them between your legs and the blood falls there. You then wash the bandages and change them regularly. I am sure your world has something like it. As for the cramps, the tea should help, and I can give you herbs to dull the pain as well."

"Thank you, Luke, but how do you know all these girl things?" she asked.

Loki stayed quiet for a few minutes before deciding he should risk trusting the child. He morphed into his female form, letting the light display it on the curtain between them. "Because I am not always male, I am a shapeshifter."

"What is your name as a girl?" she asked.

"I tend to use Lucy."

"Hello Lucy, it is lovely to meet you."

"It does not bother you that I can be either gender?" Lucy/Loki asked.

"Should it?" Holly asked. "It's just like those stories about Loki that my grandma used to tell me, he turned into a she and a horse and other things."

"Oh, did he?" Loki asked, mentally cursing himself that he had let a little too much slip to the mortal. "Finish bathing while I make us a meal. You might feel sick, but eating will do you good."

"Thank you, Lucy."

Months more passed without Loki seeing his apprentice. Out of concern, each night he searched the entire ice plains looking for any sign of the Midgardian child. He was surprised how much he missed her laughter, her addiction to learning more at every meeting. Without knowing where she lived it would be hard to track her magical signature back to the source, given the fact she was still so raw in her magic. With a few more months, he would be able to track her much more easily. For now, he could do little other than wait for her to return or pray for his help.

Loki's traditional visit to Asgard came and went, with a strong summoning from Odin to join the ambassadors from the nine realms. He loathed the constant back and forth of the bickering between the races about who got rights to what and who had stolen who's only child. The Jotun's hardly bothered in the proceedings after their annihilation at the hands of Odin. Nothing ever benefited his people, so why should they bother? Only a few diehard party people had even attended this year, barely a handful.

The final night came, with its gigantic feasting tables. Loki sat on the edge of the feast, neither wanting to 'people' nor be on show as the token Jotun delegation. Odin had pulled out the full party atmosphere, the food and drink flowing freely. Loki was not fooled by the sham laid out in front of him. Their blood bond had not survived the Ragnarök prophecy. Each time he looked at Odin, all Loki could think about was being chained to that rock with his wife trying to catch as much of the venom as possible to spare the scars that he still felt ghost pain from. Their relationship had not survived the Ragnarök reset, nor could it have been expected to. Some things were just unrepairable. She had found someone new, someone less chaotic to love. Loki would never stop anyone from gaining their own personal happiness, even if it meant leaving him alone. Loki drained his mead horn, refilling it with a subconscious touch to the scar tissue as he saw Sigyn dancing with her new husband.

Thor made his way through the crowd. "Brother! How are you?" he asked as he embraced Loki.

"Why do you insist on using that term when we are not and have never been related?" Loki asked bitterly.

"Why would I not? Are we not all siblings under the All Father?"

Loki hissed. "I wouldn't know, most father figures do not chain their fake sons to stone for centuries of punishment just for being born."

"Loki, brother, you need to let that go. It only poisons you to hold on to so much baggage from the past. Father did what he thought he must to protect Asgard and her people."

"Asgard was destroyed anyway, so go team All Father!"

"Loki," Thor admonished. "Please, go talk to your wife."

"Ex-wife, she has a new husband now."

"And you? Do you have anyone?" Thor asked.

Loki stayed silent, sipping at his mead.

"There are plenty of fine Asgardian women here, and men. Do any take your fancy?"

"I am not searching for another bedfellow."

"You can't live your life alone; our existences are far too long for that!"

"How is your little apprentice?" Loki asked, skilfully changing the subject.

"Young Holly? She is miserable, the mother figure has her locked in her chamber again. Have you not heard from her?" Thor answered.

Loki took another drink. "No, not for some time. That woman needs to be taught a lesson on how to raise children."

"The mother is Odin's favourite, to go against her is to go against Odin himself," Thor warned.

"Of course! Why am I even surprised at this juncture? Odin Oath breaker and his love of abusing innocent children. It wasn't enough to just imprison and torture my offspring, now he is going after Midgardian children as well!" Loki ranted.

"Loki," Thor warned. "This is not the place nor the time to speak like this. There are far too many ears and eyes."

"How can you defend Odin even now? You know he is a monster at heart."

Thor grabbed Loki's tunic, pulling him behind a pillar, out of direct sight of the high table. "Will you stop talking before you get yourself in even more trouble? That mead is loosening your tongue much more than is intelligent."

"She is a child! No child deserves to be locked away, neglected, tortured, and bullied! Odin needs to do better than he did with my children. All Father my ass! Some Father to the select few that he decides are worth using for his 'greater plan.' How can there ever be an excuse for allowing any offspring to go through Hel like this? Did you know that she self-harms? That she feels completely alone. That she just desperately wants to feel love. To feel that she is safe. Do you not think that a child deserves those things? That it should be a Gods given right to anyone that young to be protected no matter what?"

Thor paused, thinking about Loki's words, but did not get leave to speak before Odin's voice echoed through the halls. "Loki of Jotunheim, Lie Smith, face me and speak your poison to me directly."

The party atmosphere of the room was cut by his voice, the attendees falling silent. Music stopped mid note, the entire room turning to stare at Loki as he confidently strode into the centre of the room. Looking every inch the King he was. "Odin Oath Breaker, you are allowing one of your favoured devotees to abuse her child. A child that is a disciple of both me and Thor Odinson. A child should be free, able to learn and grow at her own rate, free of such entrapments." He was not going to back down on this, the mead was loosening his tongue, however this argument was long overdue.

Odin leaned forward on his throne to stare down at Loki like he was some insect crawling on the floor of the feasting hall. "Who are you to question the choices of a mother raising her child? It will build character. Make the child stronger overall. I fully support a mother in her parenting choices. This matter is closed and will not be discussed in the future."

Loki scowled at the All Father, blue fire starting to trickle down his body. "Really?" the Jotun spat. "You support parents' rights to raise their children? Is that so?"

"I always have Lie Smith."

"You support a parent's right to raise their children and yet you chained my son, throwing him into the Midgardian Ocean. Chaining another son of mine just because you feared his shapeshifting. Threw my daughter into the Underworld. Killing another of my sons to bind my hands before leaving me to be tortured to death. Explain yourself Oath breaker and take care in your words."

"I will not be spoken to with such disrespect in my own home. Know your place," Odin roared.

"I know my place. I am the King of Jotunheim, your equal, your advisor. The one you swore you would never drink from a cup from which I had not drunk. You swore to defend and protect all the people of the Nine Realms no matter their differences. Yet, you consistently support those who have use to you. It is me, the Lie Smith as you call me, that protects the broken, the damaged, the unloved, the alone and abandoned by the Realms. Me, who you dub the God of Mischief who makes sure these people stay alive. I support more of the Realms than you ever have Oath breaker. Explain that in front of your people, in front of all the people gathered here. Explain why you have abandoned them at their moments of most need. I, King of Jotunheim, demand your official response. Any refusal to give a full and appropriate answer will be considered a disrespect to the Crown of Jotunheim and its people. As well as war between our realms."

"Then let this be war between our people. I owe no answers to anyone. Least of all the crazy betrayer of Asgard," Odin replied.

"Betrayer am I? Crazy, am I?" Loki laughed, deep and bitter. "Oh, just you wait Oath Breaker. You will see the depths of my insanity." He clicked his fingers, opening a portal to his home. "Giants, come, we will find no aid here. This celebration of unity between the realms has ceased." His people made their way silently through the portal, 100% behind their ruler.

"Loki, are you sure that one Midgardian child is worth war between our peoples?" Thor asked. "Please, do not act rashly without thought."

Loki paused, looking at the son of Odin. "You, Thor, are always welcome on my lands. The rest of you are not. Perhaps you should think about deposing the old man to bring in fairer rule?" Loki addressed the rest of the room. "None of you here are welcome in my realm if you support child abuse and the Oath Breaker. The realm of Jotunheim is now the land of the lost and broken. Any in need will always be welcomed there. Some Father, Oath Breaker, we will meet on the battlefield soon enough." He paused again, showing the slightest form of affection towards the King in waiting. "Farewell brother."

Jotunheims Queen

Loki ducked through the portal, closing it behind him. It was time to prepare. War had come.

Chapter Five

One Last Visitation

Loki fumed to himself, pacing the snow and trying to calm himself to the point where he didn't storm back into Asgard with an army to burn the place to the ground. Nor go straight to Midgard to destroy the family of the child. As he paced, he thought he heard distant crying. "Ase?" he called.

"Luke?" he heard distantly in return.

He followed the sobs to find the child sitting in the snow with the green/gold coat he had given her, laying loose around her shoulders. "Ase, cover up before you die from the cold," he admonished, pulling the coat tighter around her frail body. "Now, tell me what is wrong? Why are you crying?"

"Mother is sending me away; I won't be able to see you anymore." She curled into her friend's chest crying.

Loki automatically held the young girl. "This should be a joyful day not a sad day. Is this not the day you turn sixteen? You would be a warrior in my Realm now. Why is she sending you away?"

"Mother says I am evil and crazy, that you aren't real, and I have a mental illness. She said that she will send me away forever and ever. So, she never has to deal with my insanity anymore. She says I ruin everything I touch. Grandmother died a few days ago, she cannot protect me anymore. Luke, I don't know what to do. I can't stop this; I am just a child."

"Ase, that woman knows not of what she speaks. I will do far more than cut off her hair for hurting you. How dare she harm my apprentice!"

"Don't hurt her, please Luke!" she begged.

"Why ever not? I could destroy her with just a single finger, she could never harm you again. Whatever you desire, speak to me your intentions and I will obey. Whatever cruelty you wish me to bestow on her, I will. Please, just speak your will," Loki asked.

"She is my mother, even if she is a bad one. I don't want you to hurt her."

Loki sighed. "Very well! I will do nothing to harm her without your permission. However, if I do not, I cannot prevent you being sent to the hospital."

Holly buried her face in his chest. "I know."

Loki wracked his brains trying to think of one last night they could have together. "I am sorry for your loss Ase, there is nothing that I say that can take that pain away. However, I can offer a distraction at least. Would you like to see the frozen gardens?"

"Gardens?" she asked.

"Come with me Ase." Loki took her hand, pulling her upright, leading her into the snow drifts. "No one has seen these, not for as long as I can remember, "he warned, "Perhaps they will not be their best anymore."

They turned, moving behind a snowdrift as a massive frozen waterfall came into view. The icicles cascading down the sheer rock face, hundreds of feet above an iced over pool. "Oh wow," Holly murmured to herself. "Oh my god, that is incredible."

"No need for such high praise, Luke is just fine for now," Loki answered automatically, forgetting she did not yet know his Godly status.

Holly didn't notice; the view was far too distracting. "Luke, this is amazing!"

Loki smiled at the mortal's excitement. "Look closer, but do not stray too close to the edge. The ice will be slippery."

Holly edged forward carefully. "What am I looking for?"

"This." Loki waved his hand, causing flowers to rise from the snow. Roses, daisies, lilies, orchids, every type of flower that you could ever think of along with a few that were native only to this realm. Flowers carpeted the snow around them as far as they could see.

"Beautiful!" she exclaimed, walking through them carefully, exploring unfamiliar blooms.

"Yes, I suppose they are. They bloom for only one day before they all return to water," he answered, wishing he could see things like she was, for the first time. "Choose one."

Holly searched around, choosing a single rose, half open. A little like something from Beauty and the Beast. "This one."

Loki plucked it, turning it over in his hands before handing it to the birthday girl. "Here, with a little magic this will never break or melt. Take it with you, use it to always remember me."

Holly gave him a hug, "This is the best gift ever."

"Did you gain any others?" he asked.

Holly shook her head. "Mother said I didn't deserve anything, only to be sent away."

Loki growled under his breath. "Well, we shall have to fix that, shan't we? No one comes into adulthood without it being celebrated properly." He would regret this when he was sober, but for now, he would be the perfect host. Taking Holly's hand, he teleported them to a long-abandoned castle. Dead flowers on the table, leaves blown in laying scattered on a floor thick with dust. The dust thick on any and every surface to be seen of what a grand building had once been. "This, Ase, was my home when I was your age. Eons ago now."

"Are you a King?" she asked.

Loki shrugged. "Yes, I guess so. Until today I never claimed that title. My people live deep beneath the surface of this realm where rivals cannot attack them. There became no need for structures like this that can be difficult to defend from the enemy. Tonight, it will host one last ball." He reached out with his magic, slowly bringing the ruin back to life, back to what he remembered from when he was young. Back when he used to hold feasts for Odin. Before the betrayal, before his people had lost everything. Loki pulled himself from the morbid thoughts, waving his hand to turn his own garments to a much more suitable green three-piece suit, and the mortal's nightdress to a lavish pale green bejewelled ballgown.

"This is like something from Cinderella." She twirled in her dress admiring it.

"I am not your fairy godmother child," he commented gently. "Do not expect me to make you a wardrobe full of these things."

"I won't," she promised.

He led her into the ballroom, green magic flickering in candle sconces lighting their way." A little more like Beauty and the Beast?" he asked. As phantom instruments started playing a tune most familiar to her. Loki took her in his arms whirling her around keeping in perfect time with the magical music.

Holly relaxed in his arms, letting the dance flow. "Luke?" she asked.

"Yes, my beloved Ase?"

"Does this mean there is a library as big as the beasts in here somewhere?"

Loki chuckled into her hair as they swung across the dancefloor once more. "One more cavernous than one of your Midgardian shopping malls. Once your dance card is full, you are very welcome to explore it."

"Thank you for the perfect birthday, Luke."

"You are most welcome, dear one."

Jotunheims Queen

Chapter Six

The Hospital Years

Loki stood alone in the silent ballroom. The party had long since ended and Holly was on her way to those wretched Midgardian Doctors. He had not been able to contact her in days, however many times he attempted to reach out. He was worried for her wellbeing. Only the Aesir knew what her future held given her toxic matron. How he wished to destroy her outright, but the time would come. He felt it. He needed to play this smart, work out where Holly was being kept. Every time he closed his eyes, all he could hear was her screams. He fought to get to her, to drag her away from this foul existence, but he could not get to her. The All Father was blocking him from seeing where the child was. He would suffer for that when Loki had built his support base, he would destroy Odin and his palace, bringing his Ase back to safety.

He looked towards the library, where mere hours(is this only hours or meant to be years?) ago the walls had been humming with laughter and song as Holly had explored his book collection. The millions of volumes that he had saved from various realms before they could be destroyed by natural disasters. He was sure he had much of the library lost from Alexandra. A Midgardian city destroyed long before remembrance. He had been drunk then, grabbing anything he could before it burst into flames. No doubt there were boxes he had never unpacked, and now would be unlikely to ever do so. Loki would never be able to set foot in this room again without thinking of that mortal child.

He stormed around the bookshelves, flicking through random books that he barely could focus on before throwing them onto the floor discarded. Spines cracked open, strewn pages torn from the cover before being scattered on the floor. He had mostly feigned sobriety for the duration of the girl's party. She had deserved at least one good thing in her miserable life. Damn that mother of hers, damn her to the deepest darkest depths of Helheim. Somewhere that he could lock her away and torture her for a few eons and perhaps after he had gained his fill for revenge, he would hand the tattered remains of her soul over to his daughter. Hel had her own special ways of dealing with troublemakers. Either way, that bitch would have an extremely unpleasant afterlife without the troublesome concerns of being reborn. Dark creatures like her did not deserve a second chance on the wheel of life. If Loki had his way, Odin would be in the chamber along with her dark heart suffering every agony with his follower. He would have Odin's head on a pole eventually when the timing was perfect.

Loki drank deeper and deeper, the rage growing inside of him until he felt ready to explode. Why did Odin always have to snuff out every light in his horrific life? What had Loki ever done that was so wrong that he deserved to be punished so constantly? That all he cared for would always be ripped away? Did he not deserve any happiness at all? Holly was his friend, his only friend and now she was gone.

Gone.

That word settled heavily in his gut alongside the copious amounts of mead. His Ase was gone. She would never come back. He was alone. When he had met her, she had given him a reason to rise from the depression of losing his family. To get up each dawn, to keep fighting. To at least attempt to be a better person.

So, damn it to Hel now.

Why even attempt to be a better person?

As the alcohol churned in his stomach something inside of Loki broke. He was not sure if he wanted to kill someone, fuck someone or burn the Nine Realms to the ground in that moment. All three sounded great options currently as he stormed up and down the library floor. Magic coursing down his arms and hands.

These books had been his most treasured possession. Kept enchanted, safe from damp, mould, sunlight, and anything else that could cause damage for his entire lifetime. His pride and joy. Gifted to someone that he cared for even more than his treasures. Now all they did was remind him of her. This was her library now and she could never set foot in it.

The injustice of it all destroyed him. The rage spiralled, hitting boiling point. Loki drained the bottle, smashing it on the floor. These volumes offended him. Loki started tearing them from the shelving. Ripping them apart. Taking out everything he felt on these fragile pages. He would not stop until there was nothing left and then, just maybe he would feel something again.

When he was done, without a word, Loki turned from the suite of rooms. Locking and barring them with a flick of his hand. They could fall to ruin for all he cared. Nothing mattered anymore, not now she was gone. He sent word to every realm that he was looking for supporters against Odin. Set his little spies to do their work. Building an army strong enough could take decades, decades he was most willing to wait. And while he did, he knew a good tavern with a strong steady supply of mead to drown out the strange emptiness he felt in his frozen heart.

It was some time, and a lot of bottles and planning later, before he heard Holly invade his dreams, begging for his help. He woke with a start, searching for her, before remembering that she was no longer there. "To Hel with this, Ase, I am coming." He opened a portal to Midgard, falling through it without even thinking to change his dirty garments.

"Loki," Thor said quietly when the figure stepped out of the portal. "You look like Hel." He took in the stained sweaty clothing and the stench of mead coming off his friend.

"It has been a long night," Loki commented.

"Night? It has been two years."

"Years?" Loki exclaimed. "How can it be years?"

Thor shrugged. "You were in your cups, I did not like to disturb you. Time moves differently on Midgard to Asgard, I thought you would have noticed that by how much Holly aged between visits."

Loki thought about it, had she aged? She must have been seven or eight mortal years old when they had first met, and just last night she had turned sixteen. He had been distracted, but two years? How could two years have passed without him even noticing since he had last seen her? "Where is she?"

"Gone where you cannot reach her," Thor said quietly. "I tried for a year or more but the Doctors keep her so highly medicated that she can barely even speak."

"Take me to her."

"You might want to change your garments first."

"Do you think I care how I look when she is in danger? Take me to her!" Loki demanded.

"As you wish, Lie Smith."

Thor led them to a small hospital, where Holly lay on a bed looking like she had been taking far too much of the good stuff. She was older, her form more filled out. She looked like a woman now, not the child he had known. There were a few books in her cell, but little else other than a bucket to do her business in. He was just lucky she was in a room with a window so he could see her. Perhaps it was Odin's idea of torture that he could?

"What has the Oath Breaker done to her?" Loki asked, staring through the window at her.

"He has tortured her, for never giving up on you. Whatever they do to her, whatever medication they give her, whatever tortures they put her through. She refuses to give up on her 'Luke.' If she disallows you, they will let her go. Until then, they will keep her like this."

"She is coming with us!" Loki fumed, heading towards the door.

"I wouldn't do that; the spell prevents any God from entering."

"Like a simple spell will stop me!" Loki snapped, before finding himself blasted across the grass. "What in the Nine Realms?" he exclaimed.

"Do you think I have not tried everything to get to her? For both of our sakes and hers, while you drowned yourself in mead?" Thor fumed. "You claim to care for her, but all you did was drink! And then drank some more until you forgot about her!"

"I swear to you Thor, yes, I drank, but I thought it had been a night, perhaps two. I have no idea where two years have gone! I would never have abandoned her!"

Thor stared at his friend for some time, before speaking. "I believe you, perhaps Odin had his say on yourself as well."

"Are you suggesting he spiked my mead?" Loki asked.

"Do you truly think he wouldn't if it kept you two apart?"

"Who is she?" Loki asked.

"Our apprentice."

"No Thor, who is she to me? Odin would never do this to a Midgardian child unless she meant something to me." Loki looked pleadingly at the tall blonde. "Who is she? What am I not remembering?"

Thor's face softened. "I can't tell you that."

"Thor, I swear to the Norns, unless you tell me I will beat it out of you."

"No, I cannot tell you. Odin has spelled me so I can say nothing. He took your memories of her and hers of you. He is torturing her to keep you both apart and stop you remembering, but you must. You need to find yourself again. Not this empty ruin the Ragnarök's made of you. Remember who you are and what is important to you. Please, for all our sakes. Remember."

"She seemed familiar that first night on Jotunheim when I first found her, but she was a child. How could I know a mortal Midgardian child?" Loki muttered.

"She wasn't always a child. We live forever or near enough, unless we are killed and even then the hands of the fates return us to the realms when we are needed. Do you think this is the first life she has ever lived?"

"We can't get to her."

"That will not always be the case."

"What did you say before, what will it take for her to get out of this place?"

"She has to forget you, to say that your time together didn't happen. That you are not real."

"Then tonight, I will visit her in her dreams and I will get her to agree to forget me. Then they will let her out, and she will be safe," Loki swore.

"And will you find her? When she is free and help her to remember you?" Thor pressed.

Loki looked over at the sleeping woman, a mere window away from him. "No, she deserves to be free of Odin's torment. I will destroy him."

"She deserves you Loki."

"No, no one deserves that."

"Loki!" Thor reached out to him.

Loki pulled away. "No, it is for the best." He vanished.

"Loki, I have never met anyone else as stubborn as you are." He gave one last glance over at the woman he was standing guard over. "Well, except for one other."

Lucinda Greyhaven

Chapter Seven

Without Her

As the years passed by, Loki found himself falling back into old habits. Getting the people to revolt against Odin was no easy matter. An attack would take time to build, prepare and campaign for. He might be the rightful ruler of Jotunheim, but the regents he had left in his stead long before Ragnarök fell were reluctant to side with him as he attempted to gain followers in his bid to war. Odin was as powerful as he had ever been. Hiding under the ice plains had become a way of life his people had adjusted to, forgetting about the spender of the above lands and the life they had once led there. Even his legendary silver tongue was not enough to gain more than a handful of followers.

Which was how he had found himself on Vanaheim greasing palms, purchasing supplies, and buying support from the elite high born. As well as purchasing himself a few more daggers to add to his collection, from the finest craftsmen in all the realms. Three passionate encounters later, Loki had gained enough wealth in supporters to move to the next realm asking for aid. There were no shortages of people in positions of power who were displeased with the All Father. A fresh Ragnarök was brewing, he could feel the rising chaos drawing him in.

Even in the midst of all of this, Loki kept finding his mind wandering to the little mortal he had not seen for a long time. The person who had started this war, his Ase. In Midgardian years, she would be well into adulthood now. The wards he had set on her mind to prevent it from cracking, also kept him out of her existence. Unless she bothered to remember him and called out for his help, he would be unable to connect with her for the rest of her lifetime. He longed to see her smile or hear her laugh again instead of the tears of their last meeting. The day that they had said goodbye. The same day that the last little soft piece of his ice-cold heart had perished. It was for the best; he would not have a Midgardian tortured by Odin simply for knowing him.

Loki was in sour thoughts, the smell of the last high born he had bedded still lingering on his flesh. A pretty wench winked at him as he entered the nearest tavern supplying him with a steady stream of mead, as well as a room and a bowl of a fish stew with a hunk of fresh bread, butter, and hard cheese. A few careful bites testing for poisons (old habits yet again after Odin had poisoned him), and he settled down to the simple meal, taking copious refills of both the stew and the mead. He allowed the strong liquor to settle in his malnourished form. Scheming left little time for food or rest. He was so invested in this upcoming war that nothing else seemed to matter, not even his own health. He knew what Odin had done to Holly (his only, dare he say the word... friend?) had been a punishment, a trigger to see what Loki would do. She had been an innocent, none of this was her fault. Just Odin's. Odin be damned to the depths of Helheim for all the heartbreak he continued to bring to all of Loki's family. Loki would take immense pleasure in plucking out the remaining eye. His mind wandered to various tortures he could enforce to gain revenge for the centuries of snake venom.

Loki was quite deep in his cups before any company approached him, as if the wenches for hire had been paid well to avoid his company that evening. Given Loki's reputation in the bedroom, he would normally be bombarded with offers. A cloaked figure sat down across from him, placing another bottle of mead on the table between them without a word. "I am a little too busy for some random 'side quest' to turn up," Loki commented, barely glancing up. "Leave the mead and find someone else to bother with whatever your tales of woe are."

A female hand reached out to grab his arm with a highly recognisable gemstone ring on show. The royal seal of Asgard. "Stay," her voice demanded.

"Fri..."

"Silence," she ordered, interrupting him. "We could both be executed for this meeting." She withdrew her hand to hide the jewel.

"Why would you even dare risk this with our peoples at war?"

"No, not our people Loki. You and Odin are at war. You will always be family to me. Whatever happens, I will not break the oath I swore to you. Now, would you share this bottle with me?"

Loki choked back a sob. "Yes, my lady. I will always share a cup with you." He opened the bottle, pouring them both a generous serving.

"You miss her, your little mortal?" Frigg asked, drinking.

"She was a dedicated apprentice; I had no complaints. She advanced swiftly, studied obediently. She would have become a master in the arts with few issues."

"I asked if you miss her Loki, not for her end of term assessment."

He sighed, knowing he was far too deep in his cups to hide his emotions under this kind of investigation. "Perhaps." His voice was thick with emotion.

Frigg laid her hand on Loki's as she topped up their drinks. "You went to war for the child, you must feel something for her?"

"A strange familiar feeling certainly, no doubt due to the torture we both faced at Odin's hand, as well as my children."

"Shh now," Frigg answered gently. "I am not here to defend my husband or any of his actions."

"Then, why are you here?" Loki demanded. "I am not going to back down over the war no matter what you offer."

"Did I say I wanted you to stop the war?"

"You will abstain from the battle?"

"I will fight at your side, myself and all of my maidens."

"You would what?" Loki stumbled out, too shocked to stay in the genteel tones he would usually grant respect to her with.

"Loki, Rightful King of Jotunheim, advisor to the house of Odin, Master Magician of Chaos, World Walker, Silver Tongue, Lie Smith, I Frigg Odinsworn offer my hand in fealty to you and your people. Do you accept that offer?"

Loki grabbed at her hand like it was anchoring him to his seat. "Do you truly mean that?"

"Odin may be my husband, but even I can admit to his faults. He had no right to do what he did to any of your children or the mortal. As a parent, he should have known better," she stated firmly.

"But why now? Why this one child?" Loki asked before he realised what she was hiding. He slid his hand over the cloak to where Frigg's stomach lay. "How far along are you?"

"A few months."

"Is it Odin's?"

"No, it is not."

"He'll kill the child if he finds that out."

"I am aware."

"You and your child will always be safe in my realm. You can pack your belongings and come forth whenever you desire, just allow me a little time to create a home for your use."

"Thank you, my lord."

"You need none of that, and no swearing loyalty to the crown or me. You have always treated me and mine with respect," he told her.

"No Loki, I let you down. I should have said no the first time he harmed your children and every time that he did after that. I regret that every single day that I live. I would like to make my debt between us right."

"Thank you, my children have missed you."

Frigg stood to leave, stroking Loki's hair in a motherly way. "Try not to fall even deeper into your cups. If you miss the mortal so passionately, find her. Odin be damned."

Loki watched her leave; she had a point. He drained the cup before unsteadily making his way to his chambers. Alone for once.

Jotunheims Queen

Chapter Eight

Rediscovery on Midgard

Loki woke in the middle of the night drenched in sweat, his heart pounding. Holly's screams echoed in his mind. She should not be able to do that. Not after all the bindings he placed on her to keep her safe. "Ase?" he called out, reaching out with his mind, searching for her. He felt the familiar barrier between them, the locked and barred door. The one he had taught Holly to create between their minds. Nothing was any different to when they had parted years before. So, why was he hearing her scream?

Loki washed, gathered his things, and threw a few coins down to pay his bill. Closing his eyes as he stepped out of the door, he folded reality to find himself on the Yggdrasil. He carefully sidestepped with his eyes closed, until he could smell the crisp snow of his homelands. He opened his eyes, finding himself staring at the long since burnt out firepit where he had used to tell Ase tales of his people. He touched the ashes which were ice cold, no one had tried to build a fire there for years. His cloak dragging in the snow, Loki swooped into the cave he had set up as their home. Two beds undisturbed, the small stash of food untouched under the stay fresh hex he had cast. His cauldron that he cooked their meals in gathering dust. Loki sighed. "Just a nightmare. Frigg got into my head."

Loki left the cave with one last wistful look back towards the campfire. "May the Norns protect you Ase, as I cannot. I hope you are happy and safe." He closed his eyes again before stepping back onto the Yggdrasil, to his next port of call. Still building his army, in the hopes of avenging his lost friend. If he had only lingered a little longer, if he had looked behind him and seen the chocolate wrapper fall to the ground that he had caught on his cloak bottom, he would have noticed the figure in the distance. He would've heard the female voice calling 'Luke' after him, but he did not. Loki left thinking he had been abandoned by someone he cared for again.

■■■

Holly woke up. "Luke?" She blinked, looking around her sparse room. "Just a dream, it's not real. Luke is not real, just a child's imaginary friend.

Luke is not real; I am just looking for a connection to the world because I am stressed out," she told herself firmly, willing her heart to stop pounding.

Sighing, she silenced the alarm beeping on her phone. Rising robotically, showering, dressing, and forcing a few sips of an energy drink down with a cereal bar as she went to work, yet another breakfast shift at the diner. She washed down her anti-psychotics with the energy drink. If she told her shrink that the dreams were back, at best case he would double her medication, at worst case he would lock her back up again. Back in that horrible, padded cell in which she had spent the last ten years. Until she had learned to start lying that it had all been for attention and Luke had never been real.

As the years had passed, even she had started to believe that it was the truth. Slowly believing the lies she had weaved trying to gain her freedom. It could not all fall apart now; she had come too far to fall back into that hellish darkness all over again. She just would not allow it. That place gave her enough nightmares as it was.

Holly looked at the pill bottle, popping a couple of extra tablets for good measure. Anything to hold her demons at bay. A short walk later and she fell into her usual work routine. Smiling a little too brightly at the customers. Polite, friendly, approachable, all the required features of a good customer service 'mask.' The same 'mask' she wore around all her co-workers and the odd brief friendship she was clinging onto to feel even slightly normal. Sometimes, Holly wondered who she would be without the mask and the medication. Or if she would just be a husk of a person, with no personality and a bunch of trauma responses.

As Holly waited tables, out of the corner of her eye she thought she saw a glimpse of a familiar figure on the street watching her but as she turned back, the figure was gone. "Get a grip, Hols," she muttered to herself.

If only that had been the end of it. As the busy breakfast service continued, the figure walked inside. Frustratingly, he took one of the service tables that she was assigned. Holly tried to ignore him as he sat there casually flicking through the menu, just focusing on her other tables.

"Holly! Why is table eight still waiting to order?" her boss (Lynda) demanded. "Get over there and take his order!"

"You can see him?" she asked in surprise.

"Holly, what the hell? Of course I can see him. Get over there or get out for good," Lynda snapped.

Holly pulled out her notepad, sliding slowly over to the table. As much as quitting was attractive given the woman constantly bullied her, staying in employment was one of her conditions of release from the hospital, so for now she would have to stay. Her eyes glued to the notepad not the man in front of her, Holly spoke.

 "Hi, the specials today are the pancake stack with maple and berries, or the egg and bacon triple stack. Can I start you with a coffee or juice?"

The man put down the menu and looked up at her. "Berries and maple please and a gingerbread latte with extra foam please."

"Thank you, I'll be right back with your order. Have a lovely day." She disappeared quickly, feeling his eyes following her around the diner. Even after she had served him his food, he was still watching her intently. "Creep," she muttered as she walked away. Still, he tipped, and tipped well before he headed back out onto the street. Holly watched him leave, shaking her head. "Why am I like this?"

Taking her break when the service ended, she dialled her therapist. "Joe? I need an emergency appointment. Can I come in this afternoon? Four? Yes, that's perfect, thank you."

 Even after the phone call, she still felt like her past was watching her. She looked out of the window as she was cleaning down the tables ready for lunch rush. Was that the guy watching her from the end of the street? No, she must be imagining it.

Jotunheims Queen

Chapter Nine

Therapy

Holly paced the floor of the therapist's office.

"I swear Joe, he was right there! My imaginary friend, not looking a single day older. Everyone could see him in the diner, he was real. It was not in my head this time. He was there. I saw him. A real live person. Luke is real!"

"Please try to calm down."

"I am calm!"

"I do not think that you are."

"I have just proven I am not crazy and that my imaginary friend is real. Why are you not listening to me?" Holly fumed.

"I am sure it was not your imaginary friend. You just saw someone who triggered a memory that had a build and frame that is like your imaginary friend or how you perceived him to be. Tall, red hair, average looks, average build, green eyes is a not uncommon description. You need to come to terms with the fact that he was just a guy, buying his breakfast and you have hyper fixated on wrapping him into your delusions. You more than likely passed him on the street at some point before your fantasy world latched onto him to pull the figure into its dimensions," the therapist said calmly.

"You mean, you think that I passed him in the street when I was seven years old, and magically years later? A whole twenty years on, he looks the same?" she commented drily.

"His father? Surgery? Really good skin care?"

"Oh, come on! Why is it easier to believe that I am insane than this could be real?"

"Why must you hyper fixate, dragging random people into your delusions? Instead of thinking I saw a man at work and he looked familiar, so I got scared and thought I saw him watching me when he wasn't there? No one else saw him other than when he ate breakfast. You imagined the rest. Luke is a delusion; he is not real. You never astral travelled to another realm. You never met a 'father figure' who taught you how to use magic. There is no better life for you. There is just cold, hard reality, which sucks sometimes but that is life. The sooner you realise that, the sooner your healing can begin. You will never be free until you can let these fantasies go."

"It was real, all of it! I saw him, it must be real," she insisted.

"Why does it, Holly? Tell me why it is so important to you that all of this is real?"

"Because if Luke is not real, then I have nothing. No one cares, I might as well be dead." Tears began falling down her face.

"Okay then, if that is your choice so be it," the therapist answered calmly.

"What do you mean?" she asked quietly through her tears.

"Would you truly rather die than give up on your fantasies?"

"I need Luke, he makes me feel safe."

"He isn't real."

Holly sobbed louder.

"Give up this Luke, leave him behind. Tell him goodbye," he pressed.

"I can't!"

"You must, or you will spend the rest of your life in a cell. Do it!"

Holly closed her eyes, trying to picture her friend's face and fighting against the tears staining her face. "I can't."

"Do it!" the therapist roared.

"Ggggood bye," she stammered.

"A hello might be more appropriate," a rich voice commented.

She knew that voice. It had comforted her for her entire childhood. Her eyes flew open. "Luke?"

The man pulled her up off the sofa and into his arms. "Hello Ase, it has been long since we last spoke." His hand brushed the tears from her face. "Did this mortal cause these?" His eyes went dark.

"Who are you? What are you doing in my office? You can't just walk in here in the middle of a therapy session and ruin a breakthrough that I have been working on for years," the therapist snapped. He fumbled for a button on his desk. "Security!"

Loki kissed the young woman's hair. "Just one moment please Ase, if you will." He untangled himself from her steel grip before advancing on the therapist, who was cowering against the wall.

"Security!" he screamed again.

Loki grabbed his throat, slamming him against the wall with a snarl. "Let me make something extremely clear, little mortal. This one belongs to me. She is my little Ase. No, she is not crazy. Yes, she did astral travel. Yes, she can do magic. Yes, so can I. And trust me mortal, if you harm her in any way ever again, I will use this knife on you." Loki materialised one, holding it at the man's throat. "And I will gut you slowly while you are still breathing. Trust me when I say that I know exactly where and how to cut to keep you alive for the majority of the process so you will still feel every single slice. Every rasping breath as you struggle for enough oxygen to fill your lungs, weighing your chest down as you bleed out internally until your puny form decides to give up fighting to stay alive. Do I make myself clear vermin?"

The therapist nodded.

"I am going to need you to use your words, or shall I start cutting to show you that I am serious in my vow? You took something that belongs to me and tortured it. I would happily do the same to you."

"Yes sir," the man answered quickly. "I am sorry sir, I was under orders sir."

"Whose orders?" Loki snarled.

"Odin."

"Odin!" Loki growled. He ran the blade's edge down the man's face, leaving a slow painful cut that would scar. "Take this message back to Odin Oath Breaker; that if he touches this woman again, I will burn down everything that he loves. She belongs to me. I will take no argument on this, touch her and you will die."

"Yes Sir," the man whimpered.

"And you, the next time we meet, you will not survive it. Now go." Loki slammed him back against the wall before releasing the mortal's throat.

The man fled from the room.

"Ase, come." Loki reached out his hand to her.

Nervously, Holly obeyed, falling back into his arms. Breathing in his scent, remembering how it had always comforted her.

Security burst into the room pointing guns.

"Time we were leaving." Loki turned his back, taking her with him as he opened a portal back to his home.

Lucinda Greyhaven

Chapter Ten

Loki returns to Midgard

Loki strolled along a Midgardian Street towards his next would-be benefactor. Pickings were slim in this realm for allies. Most of the warrior breed had died out centuries before. There were a few likely candidates in the modern recurrence of Norse Pagans, along with a handful of human mages which showed promise. An intensely small list which was rapidly reducing by the hour. He was starting to give up hope of finding anything of use here.

He stood drinking an iced coffee, dressed in a simple yet smart black longline jacket, black sweater over black skinny jeans and matching boots. Watching as the mortals scurried by in their mere lives. Some to work, others to the gym, breakfast, yoga, the school run and a million other mundane things. Loki was almost jealous of them, the effortless way that they lived their lives. So blissfully happy in their shallow little existences with no idea of the Yggdrasil or the battles that raged on for good or for evil all around them. It seemed so easy for these people. He wished for once, to be like them. No magic, no memories, no past, and certainly no Oath Breaker breathing down his neck. To just work a nine to five, come home, cook a sumptuous meal, by the Norns he had always loved to cook. Wash the food down with a few bottles of wine and then go to bed in the arms of someone who genuinely loved him for who he was. All his scars, problems and dramas forgotten. Just warm, safe, and protected in another's arms so deeply that the weight of the cosmos just fell away.

A home.

Things like that were not for villains like him. Loki absently thought about spiking his drink with something a little stronger if his thoughts were going to turn that bitter so early in the day. Or perhaps there was a bakery nearby where he could drown his feelings in sugar, he did adore the Midgardian sweet treats. So different to the food and fruits of his own realms. Oh yes, a huge breakfast of sugar, with more of this iced coffee delicacy. A little caffeine and sugar and he would be ready to face the day, and the constant need to seduce donors that he felt nothing for.

And then, he saw her.

Holly, walking by towards a diner. A little older, a little more tired looking, but undeniably her. Watching her cross the street into the diner. He lost track of time as he observed her opening, and then serving the early breakfast rush. He had to know, was she okay? Was she happy? Was she living her life like he had wanted? Did she have a lover to go home to at night? Or a cat? He liked cats, they were aloof and disconnected. Dare he go speak to her?

He must have paced on the street corner for an hour before he decided to take the plunge and enter the diner. Picking his way carefully to a table in her section of work, he vaguely glanced at the menu as she bustled around. Was she avoiding him? She never came too close to his table. Did she realise who he was?

When Holly took his order and when she brought his food from the hasty order, she seemed distracted. Like she should not or did not want to be around him. Loki felt regret at pulling her back into his screwed-up life. He threw a few notes on the table to pay for the meal, along with a generous tip. He was still royalty even if he was on Midgard, royalty act with good taste and treat their workers well.

He left the diner when Holly went into the kitchen with a tray of plates. He did not stop to say goodbye, how could he? She acted like they were strangers. Like she had forgotten him and moved on with her life. The sadness in her eyes, the exhaustion on her shoulders showed him just how much forgetting him had cost. He could not be so selfish as to force her back, risking putting her through even more just to resolve his loneliness. Not even if it broke his own heart to leave her on her own yet again.

Out on the street, Loki could not help but look back over his shoulder as she cleared his table. She looked up, locking eyes with him for a long moment. He wanted to go back inside, explain who he was and who she was. Reluctantly, Loki locked his emotions back down, burying them as deeply as he could. He turned away to continue his royal tour, collecting followers.

The entire day, whatever he did, whomever he was with, Loki found himself distracted. His mind kept wandering back to Holly and that diner. There was a rising dread inside of him. A chill working its way up his spine. She plagued his every waking thought. He knew in what was left of his ruined, blackened, cold heart that Odin was going to kill her because Loki had seen her again. It would be slow and painful. . Prolonging the inevitable until he had gained his fill of the twisted entertainment. Like an Asgardian real life version of the Hunger Games. Odin was going to make it just as painful for his Ase, as he had the rest of Loki's loved ones and family.

He drained the glass of fine wine that he was holding. Placing it on the table nearby that was covered in cheese, fruit, and various other gourmet food, he picked his way over the people writhing on the floor in various stages of undress, in this untamed orgy of decadence. Now was no longer the time to build his army, it was the time to strike. He was going to save Holly, whatever the cost. Even if it meant his own life. Odin would not take anyone else from him. This was where he would make his stand. On this pitiful mortal realm that Thor seemed so taken with. On this realm, the war would start. It seemed fitting when it had been a Midgardian girl that had started the war that his end game would also start here in this moment.

Loki took to the street, tracking that slight energy trace that he had picked up earlier. He followed it through the streets without end until he found a small building. One that looked innocent enough, yet reeked of sin and darkness. This was a doctor of some kind, and not one that helped people by the feel of it. One small invisibility spell later, and Loki found himself tracking his way through the corridors following the sound of Holly's sobbing voice.

He burst through the door, seeing the woman kneeling on the floor. Red eyes rimmed with the tears that were still freely flowing down her face. Oh, that mortal would pay for making his apprentice cry. And so would the Oath Breaker. Loki took out a knife and dropped the glamour.

Jotunheims Queen

Time to get this party started.

Lucinda Greyhaven

Chapter Eleven

Reunited

Loki pulled Holly through the branches of the Yggdrasil with him as the world walked them away from danger, his hand tightly covering her eyes to prevent any risk of her seeing something of the tree. If the mere sight risked the madness in a God, he would not take the risk of what it could do to a Midgardians' gaze. Snow crunched under their feet before he allowed her freedom from his arms. He automatically shrugged off his coat to place it around her shoulders, the thin black blouse and short skirt that she wore from the diner would do little to keep her warm here. "Ase, come. Let us find you something more suitable to wear."

Holly was rooted in place, staring at the ashes of their old ruined firepit at the entrance to Loki's cave system that they had once called home. Clearly in shock, she seemed unable to process what she was seeing.

"Ase, please come before you freeze to death. It is one thing to be here in the astral form, and a completely different one to be here in a real living body. Within mere minutes, you will fall risk to hypothermia. An hour in these conditions without appropriate garments would surely kill you." He pulled at her arm; Holly still did not move. "Ase, come or I will pick you up and carry you like I did when you were a child." He saw the tears freezing on her face. "Oh, Ase," he said, softening. "I know it is a lot to take in, but you will be fine."

Loki pulled her more firmly this time, tugging her after him into the cave. A flick of his fingers and the fire under his cauldron lit, along with the candles dotted around the cavern walls. Holly seemed too deep in shock to try and get her to change out of the wet garments, so he stoked the fire higher. Pushing her into a seated position nearby, he managed to get her out of his now wet coat, hanging it on a rock spike to dry. He exchanged the garment for a pile of furs from his bed. Holly managed to tug them around her shoulders, which was a better reaction than she had given him since they had travelled there.

Jotunheims Queen

Loki searched through his satchel for food, prepping vegetables with some dried meat of dubious origins, along with some fresh herbs into the cauldron to make a fast basic meal. Watching as the high heat that was starting to make him feel lightheaded was starting to remove the blue tinge from the Midgardians cold skin. "Ase, are you doing well?" Receiving a bare nod in response, he persisted. "Do you have any words you can use to describe how you are feeling or what is going on in your mind?" She shook her head.

This called for stronger measures. Loki reached around at the back of his food storage looking for a bottle, any bottle. There were a few dust covered bottles of mead remaining. A quick taste to make sure they had not spoiled with age, and he poured two generous horns before kneeling next to Holly and placing one in her hands. "Try and drink slowly, it is much stronger than anything you will be used to," he warned.

Holly did as she was bid, the strong liquor bringing her around from her shock long enough to look at him properly without the glassy eyed dissociation. "Are you real? Am I dreaming?" she asked.

"No Ase, you are not dreaming. I am here. You are safe. I swear upon my own life, nothing will harm you while you are here in my care."

Holly drank deeper, looking around at the cave. "All these years, all these treatments. I had given up hope." She started to sob.

Loki took her in his arms. "I am so deeply regretful for everything that you have gone through. I will swear to you a blood oath if you feel it required. You will never have to suffer through something like that ever again."

Holly buried her face in his chest, breathing in his familiar scent. "I missed you."

"I missed you too. I was lost without your guidance."

They clung together while the meal cooked, when the smell of the hasty stew filled the cave. Loki reluctantly pulled away from her to serve. He refilled their horns of mead and dished up two bowls of stew. "Eat, drink, we both need our strength."

They sat in silence as they attacked the meal and several refills of it. Holly had quite the healthy appetite now that the shock was wearing off. Although she was also downing the mead a little faster than she should do, the blushing colouring her cheeks. "Gently, that is made for a…" He bit the word God off just in time. "For someone far more used to it than you. It is strong and we have a good half a day walk before us to get to the castle."

"Castle?" she asked, confused.

"Yes, I can barricade us inside. I have plenty of provisions. You will be safe from Odin there. I can protect you."

Holly laughed bitterly. "Odin, really? The King of the Gods, the All Father of Norse Mythology is trying to kill me? Okay, I think I have had enough of this fever dream now. I'd like to wake up." She stood, swaying as the mead took effect.

"Ase, I need to be able to protect you. This cave is nowhere near strong enough to defend. I need you inside the castle," Loki warned.

She turned on him. "Ten years! It has been ten years! And you swan back into my life like it has been ten minutes! Start talking about me being in danger, and I am just meant to trust you? And allow you to lock me up in some castle away from my entire life? Away from everything I have fought so hard to get back after the hospital! I don'tt think so Luke, I am not sweet sixteen anymore. I do not believe in all this fairy tale, beauty and the beast bullshit. I am going home!"

"Ase," Loki warned.

"No, Luke. I refuse to allow you to do this to me. Take me home, right this instant."

"Holly, you are drunk. You do not know what is best for you. I won't put you in any more danger."

"You abandoned me for ten years! You told me it would be okay, and it was not. You left me!" Holly fumed. "Now, take me home and get the hell away from me. If it is another ten years before I see you again, I could not be happier."

Loki sighed, knowing this was not a battle he was currently equipped to win. "As you wish." He pulled her close to him, again covering her eyes as he moved them back to Midgard. When he dropped his hand, they were standing outside Holly's apartment. "I wish you would change your mind; this place is highly unsafe. Odin could burn it down, cause a gas leak, send a home invader. There are a million ways he could kill you in your sleep. Please, let me protect you. Come to the castle with me."

"I will do what I want to Luke, you have zero claim over me. I stopped being your apprentice years ago. When you abandoned me." She fumbled with her keys, letting herself in. "Leave me alone, you are not welcome here anymore. Nor anywhere in my life. I never want to see you again," she snapped, slamming the door in his face.

Loki sighed. "Women," he muttered to himself as he vanished.

Lucinda Greyhaven

Chapter Twelve

Regrets

Loki slammed into the nearest realm, not even caring where it was and then headed to the nearest tavern when he got there. He was starting his second bottle before he came into awareness of being watched. "What do you want, Odinson?"

"I was concerned for your welfare after you disappeared with that girl." Thor sat with him, taking the horn that Loki had poured for him. "I did not know the depths to Odin's tortures."

"She hates me for abandoning her," Loki answered mournfully.

"I am sure that is not true."

"She told me to leave and never return."

"She is hurt and confused, give her some time."

"What if she never forgives me?"

"She will."

"What if she does not?"

"Perhaps you should spend more time working out why it bothers you so much that she might not?" Thor prompted.

"She is special."

"She is that."

"A good apprentice."

"Just an apprentice Loki? You started a war with Odin over an apprentice?"

"What else could it be?" Loki's eyes narrowed. "You had better not be suggesting anything improper. She is a child. I might be a monster to your people and the whole of the Aesir, but do not dare paint me with the grotesque sin of falling for children. That will not be a fight you walk away from breathing. You know how I feel about those types of people and about children being harmed in any way."

"She is far from a child now," Thor remarked. "Should you fall for her at this age, there is nothing improper about it."

Loki glared, refilling their glasses before he struck at the other man. "She is stubborn, frustrating, and pig-headed. She will get herself killed and I will not stop it. It was her choice to return home. She refused the protection of a God, just because she is too proud to admit she needs it."

"Firstly Loki, does she even know you are a God yet or your true name? The last time I saw you two together, she had no idea what you are. Secondly, she reminds me a lot of you in her attitude traits. Maybe this is what you need, a good woman who can keep up with you and one that can stand up to you without fear."

Loki shot him a withering glare. "I will hear no more of this. She is an apprentice, my apprentice, nothing more nor will she ever be any more than that. I saw her grow up. I trained her. It would be wrong to think of her in any other form."

Thor drank deeper, eyeing the other. "It is you that keeps pressing that point Loki, not me. Trying to convince yourself there is no attraction there since you saw her in that place of eating?"

"You speak in riddles of half-truth and dramas Odinson, just like your father."

"I learned from the best 'brother,' you."

Loki rolled the cup between his hands. "I should have been there. I should have broken the magical seals and forced Odin to give her freedom. I should have built the army faster, started the war with more speed. A few years is nothing to us, I forgot how different that is for Midgardians. She has been in danger for more than half of her life, if not all of it. I never should have left her in danger. Whatever it took, I should have helped her escape her prison."

"It was too dangerous to try and free her, you were not strong enough and you may still not be. You risked her life if you stormed in there."

"I know what tortures Odin can deal out, Odinson," Loki commented bitterly. "I still remember the poison dripping on my flesh from an eternity under that serpent." He touched his chest, feeling the scars underneath the cloth. "I hate to think of someone so innocent facing a fraction of what the Oath Breaker put me and my children through."

"Perhaps, you could ask her about her time there? Listen to her burdens, share some of your own in return?" Thor suggested. "It sounds to me like it can only be understood by someone who has seen the pain."

"I would not put the troubles of an old man on the shoulders of someone so painfully young." Loki held up the horn. "Besides, I have my therapist right here."

"Loki, it would not kill you to let someone in a little!" Thor exclaimed.

"No, but it might kill them given Odin's adoration of destroying everything and everyone that I love."

"What Odin has done is wrong. I do not stand for the same values as he, but I dare not oppose him currently. I do not have the power, wealth or standing to do so openly. . I can only work in the background trying to get other Asgardians to see the truth, however that is still high treason."

"Would you stand openly against him if you did have the means?" Loki asked.

"Yes, I would," Thor replied. "I would see peace between our realms and Midgard too in our lifetimes, if it is possible. I do not share Odin's bloodlust without a reason for the battle. You are family to me Loki, when the war comes. I would take my troops and abstain from battle, rather than fight people who are kin."

"Your forces abstaining would still be a huge blow to your father's army," Loki commented thoughtfully. "You have my gratitude."

"You are welcome, blood brother. Now, perhaps it is time to leave your cups behind and find a way to repair matters with that apprentice of yours?"

"For all my silver tongue ways, I would not even know where to start."

"What does she like?"

"Books, old books."

"Then, you know where to start." Thor threw some coins on the table for their drinks, leaving Loki alone with his thoughts. Books? It was a promising idea. Not a strong enough one to repair everything, but it was certainly a place to start.

Lucinda Greyhaven

Chapter Thirteen

A Tower Moment

"They are going to make me forget you," Holly sobbed. "I am trying to hold on, but it is so hard. I feel like I forget a little more about you every single day."

Loki took her hand in his. "Whether you remember me or not, I will be here, by your side through everything. I care for you, Ase. My feelings are not dependent on you being able to see me, hear me or remember what we were to each other. I will be by your side, remember for both of us until you find your way back to me. I swear it. You will always be mine, my apprentice."

Holly woke up, her head pounding from whatever the hell they had been drinking last night. She was late for work, and not by a small amount of time. She cursed, washing and dressing as fast as possible to rush to her tacky minimum wage job.

"Holly, where the hell have you been?" Lynda snapped as she entered the diner. "I have orders stacked up so high we won't clear them until after lunch at this rate."

"Sorry, it won't happen again," she muttered, pulling on an apron to start serving plates.

"Damn right it won't. One more late, one more mess up and you are out of here."

"Yes ma'am."

Lynda rolled her eyes and went back to the remarkably busy task of flirting with the diner owner across the countertop. She did nothing other than paint her nails while Holly served the steady stream of tables solo without a break, or even so much as a drink of water until well after the lunch crowd had left. Finally, a breather came where Holly could pour herself a glass of iced tea to cool her down from the heat of the kitchen while the chef threw her a plate of something together.

"Holly, what the hell do you think you are doing? Get back to work," Lynda snapped while buffing her nails.

"No, I am taking my legally required break. All the tables have ordered and been served," she retorted.

"Get back to your work right now or you are fired," Lynda screeched.

"Here's a thought, Lynda. Get the hell off social media on your phone, stop painting your nails for twelve hours a day every single day and bus some tables yourself, long enough for me to eat something before I pass out," Holly snapped.

"Do you think I care if you are so weak that you pass out?" Lynda snarled, capping her nail varnish. "Let me make one thing perfectly clear. You are not _my_ boss; I am _your_ boss. You don't tell me what to do, I tell you what to do. I am the supervisor; you are the slave for minimum wage. Last chance, get back to work or you are fired. I have better things to do than work myself to the bone covering your tasks as well as my own."

"Working yourself to the bone?" Holly exploded. "Everyone else works themselves to the bone other than your lazy, ignorant, arrogant little ass. The only reason you haven't been fired yet and the only reason you are supervisor, is because you are sleeping with the owner. Using him like some sugar daddy to pay for your petty little desires. Do you know what the name is for a woman who sleeps with a man for his money? It isn't sugar baby, or anything that pathetic. It is **prostitute**. You are nothing but a whore."

"You are fired!" The woman's face contorted like she was looking at something disgusting. "Get your things and get out. Don't even think about asking for a reference." She drew several bills from the till, throwing them at her.

"Don't bother, I quit. I am tired of working for a pathetic little bitch who can't get anywhere in life without selling her body to the highest bidder. You are nothing to me or him. A few months' time and he'll drop you for the next busty thing that comes through the door and then where will you be?" Holly snapped. She grabbed the boxed lunch that the kitchen had put up for her. She snatched up the fallen money, before sticking her hand in the tip jar to clean it out. Not as if Lynda had done anything to earn a cut.

"Good luck in the hospital, crazy," Lynda laughed. "You know that is where you are going if you have no job!"

Holly turned back to roll her eyes at her ex-supervisor. "Another ten years in that cell is far better than another ten minutes looking at your poor cuticle care."

She slammed back into her apartment. She had no idea what she was going to do next or how long of a 'grace period' she had before the men in white coats started sniffing around. She thought about grabbing a bag, packing it and running. She had a little money saved up. She had to hope that it was enough to purchase a ticket to escape from here.

Someone knocked at the door breaking her from her thoughts. They knocked again, more impatiently. "What?" she shouted. A third knock. "Wait then!" When she checked through the spy hole no one was there, all she could see was a wrapped gift sat outside in the hall. Holly pulled open the door to check for danger, but there was nothing in either direction. Just the closed doors of the other apartments, strangers to her. Picking up the gift in confusion, she shut herself back in her room, triple locking up behind her. The ribbons pulled effortlessly from the beautifully wrapped parcel. The expensive glossy wrapping paper fell open to reveal a series of first edition Grimms Fairy Tales. All stunning covers, gilded edges, rich illustrations. The smell of old paper as she flicked through the pages. 'Regards and Apologies, Luke.' The note read in a sprawling yet elegant script.

She might be angry at him, but these books were breath-taking. Reminding her of times long gone by and a library in which they had once danced. All the dreams she had had, the broken fractures of memory surviving the therapist torture. Could all of it be real?

Holly needed time to think. She couldn't do it here. The walls of the room felt like they were closing in on her. She couldn't breathe. She put the books back down carefully on the shelf beside her bed with her few greatest surviving childhood treasures. That thin velvet box that she guarded with her life. You know when people say if there was a fire, what would be the one thing that you would grab? That was hers.

With one lingering look at the box, Holly took to the streets to try and walk off her raging thoughts, not knowing that Luke was watching her every movement, just a slight touch out of human sight to make sure that she was safe.

Lucinda Greyhaven

Chapter Fourteen

Loki's Choice.

Loki picked through the books on offer at the second-hand store. The rarer and more expensive, the better. He would have stocked his own library space if it had not been practically destroyed in his drunken rage. No doubt it could be repaired by magic in time, when Odin was not hunting the young woman. The problem was, he had no idea what Holly liked to read. The last time he had known her or what she was interested in, it had been her sixteenth birthday when she had talked about nothing other than fairy tales. A book of Grimm's caught his eye; she might be a good ten years older, but everyone liked supporting their inner child with past good memories. Right?

He flicked through the pages of the various volumes looking at the richly painted book plates. They were in stunning condition. The price tag was astronomical but he had no concerns there. He had set up a bank account and safety deposit boxes in their hundreds during his war preparations. Three more books were added to the pile. He paid for an extravagant wrapping service, before dropping them off on her doorstep. He lurked in the shadows in a nearby doorway as Holly collected the gift.

Satisfied he had made a start to repair their friendship, Loki was just leaving when he heard her door open again. The young woman rushed out into the street without looking to see who was around. She didn't look like she was in a good mood, despite the books. He felt concern clutching at his heart that he had made a mistake with his choice of books. He followed behind her as she headed up the street. It would not be long before sunset, not a time for her to be out alone. Too many things could lurk in the shadows of darkness.

Loki morphed his clothing into something more suitably Midgardian, his usual bad guy look. He walked in the shadows to be unseen as he followed. It was clear she had no set destination in mind, more like she was avoiding her own thoughts. That was something he could understand at least, although his poison of choice had always been a few bottles of whatever was strongest. Anything that could cause him to blackout as speedily as possible before a fresh set of nightmares struck. He would make a good drinking friend if that were what she required. She did not head towards the bar section of town, more towards the park. On the outskirts of which she paused to order a slice of pizza and a soda, eating it as she walked. As the sun started to creep lower in the sky, she found a bench near the water to sit on to watch the sky turning various shades of orange.

Loki leaned against a tree and observed the scene, looking for any dangers. Trying to merge in as just another casual bystander. Holly did not seem to have noticed him. He knew that she might not be all that happy when she did, but in another setting, watching the sunset together would be romantic. Loki found himself starting to become lost in thoughts of old relationships long gone by. Not so much the people he had dated, but the emotions they had instilled. That warm glow inside of love being nurtured, a warmth not so unlike the sunset in front of him. Loki felt calm, balanced in the moment he was sharing with his friend. He even moved forward to join her and admit his presence, to try to talk through all this mess they found themselves in. If he could just try to get to know her all over again. The thought of a night, or a few nights just sat with tasty food and wine, discussing the past few years like a normal pair of people had never felt so entertaining. To just fall back into the 'Luke' persona that he had created to be a part of her life.

A huge part of Loki wished that he could walk away from the 'being Loki' part of his existence. Walk from the Gods and Goddesses, from Odin's hatred, from Asgard and from Jotunheim and its people. From all his responsibilities. Just get a job, an apartment and spend his time around normal Midgardian people. Just leave behind the stress, the depression and constant state of anxiety he lived with every single day.

He was so wrapped up in his own thoughts, he almost missed seeing Odin's two ravens sat on either side of Ase on the bench. They perched on the armrests as she ripped up pizza crust to feed them. If they were here, then Odin would be close by as well. Loki drew his magic around himself like a cloak ready for action and reached out with his senses, trying to discover the source of the danger. There was a strong feeling of impending doom in the air, electrifying the atmosphere. Loki felt as if he was laid out naked in the snows of his homeland.

Holly must have sensed it as well because she stood hurriedly, scaring the birds from their perch. Either that or they realised that their task was now complete. She caught sight of him. "Why are you here?"

"I followed you," Loki commented, pulling out a blade and offering it to her.

"Do you feel it?" she asked, taking the knife.

"Odin is near, I warned you that Midgard was no longer safe for you. You wouldn't listen to me."

"I wanted to go home. You kidnapped me."

"Home?" Loki laughed. "A tiny apartment no bigger than a prison cell? A fleapit of a job, a mother who hates you and a therapist that is trying to kill you? Doesn't sound like much of a home to me."

"Says the guy who lives in a cave and drinks himself to sleep."

"This is not really the time to be bickering with the person trying to keep you alive, woman."

Holly's head snapped to the side, gasping as she saw eyes gleaming from the darkness beside them. She backed away, knocking into Loki who turned to look where the Midgardian's gaze had fallen. "Odin," he snarled, as he made out the rough form of a wolf coming towards them. "This Midgardian is mine, my apprentice. How many times must I inform you of that before you leave her alone!"

The wolf moved out of the tree line so they could see it clearly. It was far larger than any wolf from this realm, with glowing red eyes. The ravens came to perch on its wide back. "She will be mine," the wolf growled. "She was marked at birth as the All Fathers' plaything. You cannot claim what is already his." The wolf advanced, teeth bared, blood dripping from torn flesh still hanging between its' teeth. "Give up the girl and leave," it snarled. "Do not cross the All Father again if you value your existence."

"The Oath Breaker will not touch her," Loki snapped, pushing her behind him.

"The All Father will terminate her when he is done playing and you will be all alone again. I am sure we can find you another snake for company," the wolf growled.

"I said no." Loki slashed at the creature. "Keep away from her!" He shoved Holly back roughly as the wolf's teeth struck after anything it could reach. The ravens took flight, trying to peck at his eyes. Holly yelled, brandishing the knife wildly as the wolf drew blood as it bit her arm. They were heavily outgunned. There was no way to escape this situation with both still alive. Loki did the only thing that made sense in his battle-planning mind. There was only one choice he could see that would bring an outcome to them both surviving. He dropped the knife, sinking it into the wolf's side, giving him just enough time to grab Holly's wrist and opening a portal directly to his castle. He pulled her with him into the ultimate fortress.

As the portal faded away, Holly turned on her captor. "I said I did not want to be here. I said I wanted to live my life! How dare you take away my free will, kidnapping me a second time!"

"Would you prefer that I left you to be torn to shreds by a wolf?" he demanded.

"I would prefer that my wishes were respected. Take me back home right now."

"Fine," Loki snapped. For a moment she thought he would do it, before his face clouded over. "If you want to paint me as a villain in this little

Greek tragedy of yours, if you want to treat me as your jailer, your 'beast' that keeps the poor innocent 'beauty' trapped in the monster's castle, feel free! I have been demonised as a monster for my entire existence. If this is what it takes to keep you safe and alive then it is a price I will happily pay, even if it means you hating me. I am strong enough to survive your hatred for the pitiful length of your mortal life. You are not leaving here."

Loki stood panting, staring at her. He used his magic to create a few dark shadow sendlings. "These will cater to your every wish, fetch you anything you need while you are imprisoned here." He shook his head at her. "I thought that you were different to everyone else. I thought you were better than them, or I would not have bothered wasting so many years taking care of you. I should have just killed you that first night you barged into my home, child or not. It would have prevented so much. You were not worth my favour. I could have picked any Midgardian, not a fool."

He looked ready to burst into tears. Holly reached out a hand to him but he stepped away effortlessly, a perfect mask of indifference on his face. "Take the staircase up, and follow the corridor to the right, straight until the end. You will find suitable chambers there. The sendlings will bring you food and clothing. You have no need to be bothered by my presence there. The castle is far large enough to encompass both of us without ever having to meet. I do not even have a west wing to ban you from, nor a rose wilting away. I bid you goodnight, child."

Loki turned away, vanishing before she could respond, leaving Holly alone in the entrance of the grand building.

Jotunheims Queen

Chapter Fifteen

Trapped in the Castle

"I thought you were different."

Loki was hurt. All he had been trying to do was protect Holly. Yet again, he found himself hated for trying to do the right thing. Story of his life. It was not hard to be villainous when everyone treated you like you were one. He made himself invisible, striding to her room at speed to get there before her. Wasting more magic than he had any right to use when he was weak, to prepare anything he thought she might have need of, to be comfortable for a few days while he rested. He could rethink after that, or send a sendling to ask what she wanted. He faded into the shadows of the window when she entered to explore. Once he heard splashing making it clear she was bathing, and he was safe to move, he set out a meal, striking his magic into the fire to light it. One last glance around the room as he left, he wished that things were different. He wished that he could stay and they could dine together like they once had. Those days were gone forever, she only saw him as a beast now. Her monstrous captor for the time she had to remain at the castle.

Loki found his way back to his own chambers, sealing the door with magic behind him. Alone at last, Loki allowed the full weight of his whirling emotions to hit him. All he could focus on was her angry, hurt face. He felt the tears coming before he could choke them back down. He slid down the wall, letting the pain roll over him. His heart was broken. Odin always had to ruin everything. Couldn't he just have one cordial thing in his life without the entire Nine Realms conspiring against him?

∎∎

Holly tried following Luke, but with him vanishing there was no way of knowing what way he had gone. The corridors seemed endless; it could take weeks to locate him in this, even if he stood perfectly still all that time. Her head hurtand her arm throbbed from the wolf bite. There was blood soaking through her torn sleeve. Tired and aching, Holly made her way upstairs. With each step she took, candles lit in the wall sconces to light her way. The only door ahead that opened for her led to a slightly dusty set of rooms. There was a grand sitting area with a desk piled high with books, a window overlooked an ice-covered mountain top. An internal door led to a further imposing space with a four-poster bed piled high with furs dominated the room. Closets full of women's clothing stood at the far end of the space, all in her size. Everything had been catered for her, even down to silk and lace underwear and thick winter nightgowns. When had Luke set up a full wardrobe for her? Yes, she was used to him creating the odd garment for her as a child from his magic, but a spread this large must have been exhausting. A noise from the corner of the room led her to discover a third doorway, leading to a vast bathing chamber with a sunken bath. Floating candles, flower petals and herbs lay on the surface, the water set at the perfect temperature. "Luke? Are you here?"

She sighed when he didn't answer, he must have been there. How else had everything been set up for her stay? Or was it always set up for when a guest appeared, and the sizing was sheer luck? It was all too confusing and overwhelming. Days ago, she only had to worry about her idiot supervisor, now she was trapped in a castle.

She stripped off her blood-soaked clothing, throwing it into what appeared to be a clothing basket. She lowered herself into the bathtub. It felt amazing. The warm bubbly water relaxed some of the tension from her body. She attempted to clean the wound on her arm. It already looked nasty, like it was trying to grow an infection even though it had happened barely an hour before. She washed it again, trying to use a damp warm towel to draw out anything that could be causing the infection. It worked to an extent but it hurt, she could barely raise her arm as she towelled off and changed into one of the night gown and robe sets.

A fire had been lit in her living area while she bathed, while a tray of cheese, fruit and breads had been left on a table. Even wine and water had been provided. She picked at the food, not having much of an appetite despite barely eating for days. The pain in her arm was far too distracting. She would trade the whole spread in an instant for a bottle of pain medication and a tetanus shot.

Once Loki had recomposed himself, he went back to check on his 'captive' covered by the invisibility glamour. The first thing he noticed in the suite was the barely touched meal. Mostly unsurprising given it was her first in a new, strange place that she didn't want to be in. However beautiful the cage was, it was still a cage unless Holly could adjust her mind to see it in a kinder light. If she ever could. Midgardians had such short lifespans that he would not wish her to exist for all of it in misery. He hoped that when he killed Odin, she would be able to have a slice of her mortal life free from fear. She had been through enough already with everything else she had endured. If she ever stopped hating him, he would like to show her the rest of the Nine Realms.

He cleared the plates away before discreetly looking around the bedroom door, not wanting to see anything he should not. It was by the luck of the Norns he thought to do so given what was waiting. "Holly!" He dropped the glamour, rushing to the side of the bed. She was sweating, her skin grey, cool to the touch. "What happened?" he demanded. His gaze fell to the blood-stained towel badly wrapped around her arm. He pulled it off, removing flakes of skin with the makeshift bandage. The wound was clearly poisoned. Odin's last laugh. He cursed himself for allowing himself the weakness of emotions instead of making sure these wounds were healed. He should have remembered that the wolf had bitten her while the ravens went for his eyes and insisted that it was professionally cleaned before they parted, fight or no fight.

Loki pulled out a package of medical supplies from the bathing chamber that she had clearly not located. Cleaning the wound slowly, he picked out what looked like shards of the wolf's teeth. Once the blood and gore was gone, he could see what he was working with. He was already close to exhausting his magic core from preparing the room and the battle. This would take every ounce of his will power. He pulled the faintly flickering core of blue magic into his hands, willing it down into the wound to flush out the toxins and repair what he could. He found small bruises, cuts and a chipped bone. He healed as much as he could before his flame burnt out, as any mage only had so much magic to use before they needed to rest, recharge and feed. Loki had been running on the edge of empty for centuries, trying to will himself not to black out, he changed the bandage. The dregs of the wound could heal naturally now.

A wave of exhaustion hit him as he attempted to stand, and he muttered a string of Norse curses to himself. He looked for any reserves of energy, just enough to get him back to his own chambers. His last thought as he collapsed was worry for Ase before all he saw was darkness.

Jotunheims Queen

Chapter Sixteen

Escape and Tolerance

Holly's sleep was peppered with nightmares of wolves stalking through the darkness towards her. She awoke to what sounded like wolf howls that she couldn't quite tell if were from her dream or from outside of the castle gates. Her second thought over the noise of her pounding heart was for Luke as she saw his crumpled body on the floor by the bed. He was unharmed and breathing when she checked, just deeply asleep. She realised it was one of the few times that she had ever seen him sleeping.

As she climbed out of the bed, another thought crossed her mind. That her arm was feeling much better. Looking down, she realised it had been recleaned and bandaged. Luke must have done it while she slept. Holly slid onto the floor next to him, but he clearly was not going to wake anytime soon. The position he had fallen in looked quite uncomfortable. He was tall, lean, yet strangely heavily built, leaving her unable to move him. All she could do was nudge him into a slightly more comfortable position, shove a pillow under his head and cover him with the furs.

She bathed again, teaching herself how the water system worked before dressing in the simplest garments she could find in her wardrobes. She chose a trouser and shirt set, not unlike Luke's normal preferred garments. They looked far more comfortable than the ornate gowns and medieval type dresses that made up much of the room. Her arm was healed now, although a little stiff when she tried to move it.

Discovering she had a renewed appetite, she made her way down to the kitchen to make a little food for both of them. She was moved out of the way by the strange shadow creatures he had created as they set up two trays of the palace staple foods of meat, cheese, bread and fruit. She was allowed to eat hers in the kitchen area, before taking the spare tray up to Luke. She left it by his sleeping form as she went to explore.

At least if Luke was sleeping, she had a hope of finding a way to escape without him noticing. Row upon row of bedrooms greeted her on the upper floors, covered in dust sheets with bathrooms that had clearly not been used for decades. Luke seemed to have only opened the rooms that were in use at the time. There were a suite of rooms in the tower which were still locked to her, which she took to be his personal quarters.

Downstairs, she found the ballroom door still open with the remains of her 16th birthday decorations still ghosting the walls. It felt like a lifetime ago, so unreal compared to everything that had happened since. A young girl in a pretty dress dancing with her best friend. There had been such an innocence about that time, an innocence she wished had remained. Instead of her being the jaded creature the hospital had turned her into.

She couldn't help herself from trying the door to the library, the most vivid memory she had of that time. The never-ending walls of books that reached tall enough to meet God himself. She could spend the rest of her life in there reading, and still never get through more than 2% of the books contained within those walls. It was the only thing that might make this imprisonment bearable. The door was disappointingly locked. She rested her hands on the door, wishing she knew the right magic to pick the locks. Working her way around, she came upon a dozen more locked doors including the front door that was not only locked, but barred with a log of wood she could never even attempt to lift.

As an escape plan went, she was failing miserably. She did locate a room of potions or a sort of spell room. The bottles were labelled in a language that she could not read, as were most of the books. The crystals were interesting. She made a pile on the floor of the ones that energetically called to her, sitting with them while looking through a crystal guidebook. She found another volume that she pored over the illustrations of the realm she was now in. The star charts were interesting, vastly different to what she knew of her own world. Finding paper and a quill (what a strange, old-fashioned way to write!) she practised until she could make notes of how these stars differed to her own, from the distance memories she had from her school lessons.

Loki slept like the dead, his power completely drained. Odin could have beheaded him in that state of slumber, and he would never have heard a single footstep. He would have to be more careful to not sleep around enemies, even if it was difficult to think of his Ase as one. He struggled his heavy eyes open, pulling himself upright. His back hurt, more than a little. He popped it back into place as he stretched. He needed to bathe urgently to restore his muscles. It occurred to him that he had been provided with a pillow and blankets along with a fresh meal, a kindness he had not expected given the circumstances.

Holly was gone. She couldn't leave the castle so that was of no importance. He ate hurriedly, wanting to be gone before she arrived back. He had just enough magic returned to clear away the plates. Stiff and limping a little, Loki made his way down the corridors looking for the Midgardian. There was a motion and was that humming? Coming from his spell casting chamber. He found Holly cross-legged on the floor, surrounded by papers and books. "Still quite the scholar I see," he remarked.

She looked up from her work. "Not really, but the library was locked and every door to anything interesting. Like freedom! So I was bored. I can't read any of them."

The library! Loki's heart grew heavy. Of course that would be one of the first places she would try to visit. He would have to try and repair the books before she realised what destruction his grief had caused. Always the master of misdirection, he looked through the drawers and found an old pair of spectacles that he was not sure who they had once belonged to anymore. Bending them gently in his hands to fit her smaller frame, he muttered words of a spell and offered them to her. "These should help you read most of my books. Not any of the dangerous ones, but enough for you to continue with your training if you so wish."

She reached out and took the glasses, trying them on as the words moved into focus. "Thank you."

"You are welcome." Loki went to leave the room, pausing in the doorway. "Do I need to lock away the poisons to prevent you doing anything foolish to either of us?"

"No, you have no need to worry for either of our safety currently," she answered dismissively, more interested in her new books than his company.

Loki nodded. "Please inform me if that situation changes in anyway. It would be bothersome to have to travel to the underworld to return your soul to its flesh."

Holly glared at him for interrupting her reading. "How long am I forced to remain here?"

Loki looked down at her with compassion. "Until I can guarantee your safety."

"I never asked you to protect me."

"However, you will still gain my protection. Give me a little time and I will return to you as much freedom as I can safely risk doing," he promised. She did not answer, he could feel her rising anger towards him. "I will send your meal to your room with the servants. I will not put you to the trouble of suffering my company in the dining room. Be safe Ase." As an afterthought, he added a pile more books to her collection. "This realm's history, it might help you to learn about the place you are to become Queen of. "

"Queen?!" she exclaimed.

"Yes, becoming my Queen is the easiest way to make Odin back off. Then you will have the protection of all of my people."

"I am not going to be anyone's Queen, let me make that extremely clear! You are not going to kidnap me and force me into your bed."

Loki looked confused. "Bed? What does being the Queen have to do with my bed? It is nothing more than a simple business deal for your safety. Marriages stem from one party supplying the other with something of use. Money, fame, power, land, or in this case protection. When Odin is dead, we divorce and go our separate ways. No part of that requires you to ever share my bed."

"You are a freak." The good humour from her glasses was exhausted by his new revelation. "Marriage should be for love and companionship, not power and wealth. I repeat, I will never marry you or be your Queen. Not ever!"

"Oh Ase, why must you always be so difficult."

"Maybe because you keep trying to control me and force me into things that I want no part of!"

"As I said to you yesterday, I will do whatever it takes to keep you safe. Even if it means your hatred. Goodnight Ase." Loki stormed out of the door. Why was she so frustrating whenever he tried to do something nice!! He needed a drink, a bath, and then maybe he could think of a way out of this situation.

Lucinda Greyhaven

Chapter Seventeen

Grudging Cohabitation

They fell into a routine over the next few months. Loki would rise early, doing any spell work he needed to do before leaving the room free for Holly's researching, while he stayed in the library writing the letters he needed to, and slowly started to repair the books. He would eat before she rose and late in the evening after she had returned to her chambers. Every so often, Loki would feel the wards ping as she tried to force open a door or window. Now and then he even heard what sounded like the scratchings of a lockpick at the door while he was working. She was persistent, he had to respect that. They had not spoken since that day he had mentioned he would make her Queen. Her reaction confused him; most women would love to be Queen of their own realm. To have access to all the treasures of the realm and all the rewards of being a Queen. He had not asked anything in return for her to react in such an aggressive fashion. They easily avoided each other, neither wanting to rehash the events.

A few hundred books had now been repaired, although it seemed like several thousands more still awaited his attention. He regretted his drunken actions that had brought them nothing but harm. If he had not gone on a rampage, Holly would be having a far more pleasant time enjoying this paradise of literature, rather than the dry textbooks on magic from his chamber. She must need a break from all that learning. Loki looked up at the clock on the wall, the candles had burnt low. His neck ached from being cramped over the table working. The evening hour was late, Holly should have retired to bed by now. He locked the door behind him, heading to fetch a book on herb craft when he realised she was still studying inside. "My regrets, I will return later." He thought he saw a hilt of one of his daggers sticking out of her pocket, interested that she was thinking of arming herself. Impressive, that and her constant attempts to escape the castle. She showed no sign of stopping her attempts. He had caught her once, prying open the shutters of a window in one of the spare bedrooms with a table knife, not realising he had spelled the air in front of the windows into a barrier she could not escape. Her utter frustration, slamming the shutters closed again when she realised there was no escape that way. She had even knotted spare bedsheets into a rope to lower herself to the ground, how very 'Belle' of her. The name suited her well, she had certainly grown into her looks in adulthood. Her curves filled out his laced shirts as she stubbornly refused any of the gowns he had provided her. He had stolen away again, before she had realised he was there.

Holly barely glanced at him. "Do as you require, I am just studying a map of the Nine Realms as your Yggdrasil describes them."

Loki glanced at the book. "Frigg gave me that for my children to read. Is it too basic for you? I could find something more complicated if you desire?"

"Frigg? As in wife to Odin?"

Damn it, Loki cursed to himself. So much for keeping 'Loki' a secret identity. "Yes, that Frigg." He tried to play it off as nothing.

"And Odin, King of the Gods and the All Father wants me dead?"

"Yes."

She sorted through a pile of books beside her. "I asked your shadows for some books on Odin, they can get into the library when I can't."

Trust Holly to find a loophole around his enchantments. Her grandmother had aptly nicknamed her 'Lady Loki'. Still trying to play a vague disinterest in the conversation, he spoke again. "Yes, my regrets. The renovations are taking a little longer than I expected. A few more weeks, perhaps a month and you will be free to explore it. The sendlings or I can fetch whatever you require until then. Or if you have any requests, I can go purchase the books for you. If you do not wish to ask me directly, I understand. Just leave a list here on my desk and I will fetch it in the evening. Perhaps old Midgardian poems? Or do you prefer fiction? A good romance would normally be enjoyed by someone of your age, perhaps some Arthurian legends?"

Holly stubbornly held out one of the books, showing a drawing of Odin and Loki drinking a wine horn together with the words 'blood brothers' scrawled underneath. "Your name isn't Luke, is it? You are Loki, Lord of Jotunheim, master of magic, and so on and so on. We are on Jotunheim, and Odin hates you because of Ragnarök."

Loki's shoulders fell, there was no hiding his reaction this time. The weight of the entire Nine Realms seemed to have settled on his shoulders this fine evening. "Yes, I am he." There was no point in denying it, Holly would not have dropped the subject until she had found a way to prove her point.

"Would you care to explain why you lied to me for half of my life that you were just a wizard called Luke?" she asked coldly.

Loki leaned heavily against the desk. "Can I at least offer you a drink in the dining room? I know I need one before this conversation."

"That would be acceptable."

She took his offered hand to help pull her up from the floor, shoving the blade deeper into her pockets. He would have to watch that, although he knew his reactions were fast enough to avoid her attempts should she attack him. With perfect manners, Loki offered his arm for her to take, a little surprised when she accepted. He led her across the hall to the dining room. He poured her a glass of the best wine, which she left untouched. He drained a glass, before pouring a second trying to locate the correct words to explain the greatest lie he had ever told. "Did you read all the mythology? Or just the part where Odin and I swore our blood bond on the battlefield."

"I read from your first meetings, to Ragnarök and everything in between."

"That is good. The mythology is biased, but it gives a grounds of understanding," Loki answered. "Odin and I, we don't exactly agree completely. We have not for a few lifetimes now, longer than I can remember. I regret that Odin has dragged you into our little squabbles."

"Why didn't you tell me who you were?"

Loki refilled his glass, finding it empty again. She still had not touched her glass. "Ase, you were a tiny child. I had just come from arguing with Odin over territory for my people. I did not know how much your grandmother had told you of the old ways. I did not want to frighten you if you saw me as a monster."

"Yet, you still lied as I grew up."

"I did not want to risk our friendship. You treated me like a person. There was no fear in your eyes of the Lie Smith. Do you have any idea how long it had been since anyone had treated me like a person? Not just Odin's monster."

Holly motioned for him to continue.

"I was planning to settle up my affairs, give over the throne to my second in command and hole myself up in that cave forever until-," Loki paused to get his emotions back under control. "Before I met you, I did not want to live anymore. I haven't admitted that to anyone."

Holly must have found the answer acceptable as she moved to a fresh question. "In the hospital you still didn't tell me. Why?"

Loki laughed bitterly. "I did tell you."

"You did not."

"May I touch you, there is something that I should show you. You might as well hate me for the full list of my crimes rather than just the highlights."

Holly held out her hand.

"Drink your wine, this will hurt." He took her hand, closing his eyes as he looked for the memories he had blocked.

"Loki, Loki where are you? I am all alone. Loki, please! Save me."

Holly pulled back. "What was that?"

"Shh," Loki said, taking her hand again. "Don't fight it."

"I'll remember for both of us."

"Ase, before you decide if this is what you want us to do. You need to know who I truly am."

"Loki, I always knew."

"How?"

"I wouldn't be here if I didn't trust you."

"Odin will kill you if you don't let me go."

"I don't care."

"I do. I won't have you die for me. Please, let me do this to keep you safe."

"Never."

"Please Ase, for my sake."

"I don't want to lose you."

"It won't be forever. I'll come back, when it is safe. I'll remember for both of us."

"You better come back for me."

"I swear it on my life, I will come for you when it is safe."

Loki let her hand slide out of his, the barrage of emotions and memories battering at his mind. "I am sorry for your pain," he said hoarsely.

"I agreed," she said quietly.

"You agreed. I am so deeply regretful for that day, but it was the only way to keep you safe. I could not break the wards that Odin set on the building. It took every piece of power I could beg, borrow or steal just to break into your dreams. I could only wait and hope that if you forgot about me, Odin would get bored with you. That in time they would set you free and you might find something in your life to care for. To find joy in again without me tainting everything."

Holly slapped him as hard as she could across his face. He did not flinch; she could take her anger out on him however she saw fit. "If you ever call yourself a taint or a problem in my life again, my next slap will be somewhere far more sensitive. I am short, everything you prize so much is directly at my level to hit."

"I understand." He did not move, allowing her to make the next move. He fully expected her to walk out of the room, never speaking to him again.

"We also need to talk about the fact that you keep referring to me as 'yours'. I am not nor will I ever belong to any man. Least of all you."

"Saying you belong to me is an issue?" he asked, confused.

"Yes, it makes me sound like your slave or something. Or like you are a possessive ex-boyfriend."

Loki ran the idea through his mind for a few moments. "That is not what I mean by that word."

"Then what do you mean?"

"I am a person of standing, meaning and power. By referring to you as 'mine' it means you are shown reverence and respect by those around me. That the respect shown to me, should also be shown to you. It is a mark that you are unquestionably under my protection. That should any harm come to you, there would be retaliation or even war between the parties. If I did not refer to you as 'mine' how do people around me know that you have my blessing? We will not be in this castle together forever, people we meet must know not to mess with you when I am not around."

Holly sighed. "I guess it is something I can learn to tolerate."

"My thanks Ase." He nodded. "Is there anything else we should discuss? Any more wrongs I can put right? Or any ways to pick the locks or escape the castle I can suggest that you have not already tried? Should I suggest another cache of daggers for you to plunder?"

"You know about that? All of it?"

"I do."

"You are not upset by it?"

"I would be more concerned had you not attempted it. Keep the knife, at least you will be able to defend yourself should anything happen to me," Loki answered. "Any other issues of business for tonight? I confess I am exhausted, it has been a long day."

"I think I am good for now," Holly said. "Let me be clear, we are not good. I do not want to be locked up as your prisoner."

"Nor do I wish to keep you confined. I have great fears of what Odin will try next if I let you out of my protection sphere."

"Odin is an asshole," Holy replied, taking the wine bottle from the counter to refill both of their glasses.

"Excuse me?" Loki stumbled out, not believing he had heard the words he thought he had.

"Odin is an asshole," she repeated. "He breaks his promise to you that he'll never drink from a cup that you hadn't already drunk from. He imprisons your children, scared they will kill him at Ragnarök therefore creating Ragnarök. Poisoned you under that weird snake thing. Killed your son, bound your hands with his body parts. Disgusting by the way, what sick fuck does something like that to a kid? And yet somehow still manages to spin the story to make you into Lucifer while he gets away with everything. That is bullshit and frankly, if that is what survived in mythology after countless translations, I am in no doubt that far worse done to you has been forgotten about. I seriously hate to think what else he could have done to you. Are you ok?" She paused in her rant when she realised that Loki was softly crying.

"You see me. You truly see me and Odin for what we are."

"Luke." She paused to change the word. "I'm sorry this is going to take a little time. Loki. What happened to you and your family was not your fault."

"But how do you feel about things like me cutting Sif's hair or getting Balder killed?" He could not hold out hope for full redemption from her.

"Perhaps if they had not been so arrogant and vain, you wouldn't have needed to show them the error of their ways. It was hair, not the end of the world. As for Balder, you didn't pull that trigger. You just suggested the arrows construction. It is not your fault."

Loki looked close to completely breaking apart. "Ase, please do not say it if you do not mean it."

"I do mean it," Holly insisted. "I never say anything I do not mean. You got screwed over, it is not your fault. I will say that as many times as you need to hear it." She laid a hand on his arm in comfort. "It won't always be this shitty, I promise. You'll make new friends and find someone who loves you. Do you like women? Or men? Or both?"

"Thank you," he choked out. "Are Midgardians so open with their sexuality now?".

"You are welcome, Loki," she answered. "Yeah, hell yeah! We don't care who you love as long as it's legal and consensual."

"I like both, Odin doesn't like that either."

"Oh, we have a word for that. It's 'Homophobic'."

"What does that mean?"

"That Odin is an asshole."

Loki laughed. "You keep calling him that."

"Because it is true!" Holly replied with a smile. "I'll leave you to your wine, but let me be extremely clear to you. You ever tamper with my mind or my memories again, I will make you regret it."

Loki found himself laughing. "Somehow Ase, of that I have no doubt." He wiped his eyes, turning back to the wine bottle as she left to calm his nerves. Maybe being trapped in the castle with Holly would not be so bad. Perhaps it could even start to become slightly pleasant to have a friend around. A real friend.

Lucinda Greyhaven

Chapter Eighteen

Weapons Training.

The next day dawned with a brighter sense of purpose. A freedom that Loki did not know he had been devoid of. His habitual early breakfast and long hours repairing books did not feel as droll as it normally did. His back aching from his work, Loki went to the kitchen to fetch something to eat. On his way back, he found the door to the armoury open. How strange, he had double locked it by both key and magic. The sendlings could enter, but they would have no need of a door. Only a person with physical form would need a door, and of that there were only two in the castle. A half-eaten bread roll in his hand, he came in with dagger drawn to find Holly throwing daggers at a target and mostly missing. "Do I have to worry about you murdering me in my sleep now, Ase?" he asked. "I said you could keep the single dagger. One blade, not steal my entire armoury. I do have need of weapons to defend us."

Holly looked back at him. "It looked a lot easier in the movies, and I stole nothing. Your daggers are all still in this room."

"Well Katniss, knife throwing is all about the wrist. Strong wrist, strong throw." He took a seat to finish his lunch while watching her train. "Or would you prefer to be Tris, first jumper?" He checked his daggers, mentally counting how many were missing compared to how many lay in or around the target. "The other five better return to this case when you are done," he warned. "I will search your pockets."

"How do you know about Midgardian young adult dystopian movies?" Holly asked. "Five? I know nothing about five missing blades."

Loki shrugged. "I watch many movies. I like cinemas with fresh salted buttery popcorn. I should be asking how you watched so many films in a hospital?"

"We had a weekly movie night if we behaved, but I read them as books first."

"And they spent that one night showing teenagers movies and allowing them access to books about teenagers rising up against their oppressors?" Loki queried.

"When you put it like that!" she laughed.

"Are you hungry? I could fetch the sendlings to feed us?" he offered.

"I'm not hungry thank you, but please don't let it stop you from eating," she answered, badly throwing another knife.

"Shoulders square to the target, one foot in front of the other, slowly, feet far enough apart to keep your centre of gravity, bend your knees slightly. Focus, calm your breathing and then throw," he suggested.

"Okay 'Four', why don't you show me how it is done," she demanded, glaring.

Loki materialised a knife, throwing it at the target without looking while eating, still managing to hit it dead centre. He was showing off and he knew it.

"How did you do that?"

"Centuries of practising and cut fingers," he replied. "For a new starter, you need to know the weight of your knife, the distance to the target, wind factors, and so many different things can affect how the knife moves through the air. You need to keep the stance correctly. With practice and time, you will learn to calculate all the variables in a split-second while both yourself and your target are moving. Warriors train from an early age to master the skills before they move onto swords and other weapons."

"Could you please teach me?"

"Why do you want to learn?" he asked, brushing away the crumbs of his meal. "I will not take it as an excuse to keep pilfering my weapons."

"If Odin is after me, I would feel safer if I could defend myself even in a small way. The swords were too heavy for me to lift, most of your weapons were. The bow is too cumbersome to carry. So that left the staff and the knives. Without wanting to walk around like Gandalf the Grey, the knives remained as the only sensible option as well as being easy to carry."

Loki nodded. "A logical path of thought, extremely warrior-like. Seeing the problem, and then making the logical steps to resolve it. I am impressed. I am also impressed that you gained entry to a room that was locked by key and magic. Care to explain how you got into my armoury?"

Holly dropped the knives back onto the bench. "Am I in trouble?"

"Not if you explain the trick."

Holly pulled a hair grip from her ponytail. "I picked the lock."

Loki took it, turning it over in his hands. "Such a simple item, learned by wanting to escape the hospital no doubt."

She nodded.

"And the magical lock, how did you bypass that?"

"I asked it nicely. I saw you put weapons away in here. So, I asked the door if it would allow me entry for reasons of self-defence."

Loki closed his eyes, checking every ward he had placed on his home. She was telling the truth. The castle had decided she was worthy of entry and its trust. He opened his eyes to look at her. "You would make a fine Queen of Jotunheim."

"Excuse you, don't start that again!"

"Ase," Loki hissed. "Once again, I remind you that marriages are born of wealth, power and alliance of houses, not bodily functions and love as you seem to feel. It would just show a deeper kinship than a friendship, or me being your tutor. Do you think that I fucked Odin when we swore our blood bond?"

"Eww, I hope not. Surely you have better taste in lovers or are the pickings so slim on Asgard?"

Loki chuckled. "I'll have you know, that I have not taken a lover for any reasons other than alliance for," he paused, trying to count, "I do not think I even know how long." He focused back on the Midgardian. "If the idea of a protective marriage is so appalling to you, please forget my comments with my apologies for suggesting you could be wed to someone so monstrous, and I will take my leave of you."

Holly, put a hand on his arm to stop him from leaving. "Look. I am trying here. I just don't belong in this realm of yours. I am trying to tolerate being referred to as 'yours' like I am just some piece of property. The idea of being some fake Queen is not appealing, it is not an insult towards you."

"It would not be a false title," Loki muttered. Changing the subject before it devolved into another fight, Loki walked over to stand behind her, adjusting her body position towards the target. "Now, for your blade. You can hold it in a 'hammer' grip like a fist, like my brother would throw it. Or a 'pinch' grip of two fingers like I do. A hammer gives you more power, a pinch more precision. You have not a great deal of strength yet in your arms, which will come in time. Bring your knife arm, this elbow here to the level of your earlobe. Steady your breath, focus and then let the blade fly."

Holly followed her tutor, his body moulded to hers. The blade landed just an inch away from his at the centre of the bullseye. "YES!!!"

Loki nodded his approval. "You are a natural, are you sure you have never done this before?"

She shook her head. "Only what you showed me as a child."

"If you are serious about training, there is a course outside in the courtyard. If you are going to practise, you will need to train your body to be stronger just like our children do before they start weapons training. I could remove the locks on the kitchen door, resealing them on the borderline of the castle gates to allow you to live more freely. You would have to reassure me that you will not try to break out from the new boundary line. Would that be acceptable?" he offered. He realised their bodies were still melded together in a position that was almost sexual, so he stepped back to allow her room to breathe. He couldn't deny it had been enjoyable to be so close to her, clearly he needed to take better 'care' of himself if he was being turned on by helping his apprentice train.

"I would love that," Holly enthused at the idea of going outside. Feeling the sun on her skin, or even the blistering snow would be something after all this time. She pouted slightly as he moved away, reaching out a hand to snag him back closer that he ignored.

"Just be gentle with your body, eat well and try not to cut off any of your body parts or mine while you study." He felt the urge to take her back in his arms and train with her, to smell her hair and bury his face in her neck. Loki sighed. He needed to get laid and get these foolish ideas out of his head. He didn't like her that way, he couldn't possibly. Thor had just put foolish ideas in his head.

"Promise."

"And touch none of the knives in the purple box, the blades are coated in fast acting poisons."

"Ooh."

"I said no."

"Damn it."

"Who would you use them on?"

"My mother."

"Tempting."

"Odin."

Loki laughed. "Oh Ase, that I would like to see one day."

"Then you shall."

Loki stood. "I have things to do. I need to travel to Midgard for supplies tomorrow and to pay the rent on your apartment for a few more months. Is there anything you need while I am gone?"

"Some of my clothes, and there's a black velvet box on my desk. I need that urgently please."

"Understood. Anything else?"

"Can I come with you?"

"I am sorry."

"I understand. I don't like it, but I understand."

"I will return your freedom to you as soon as I can resolve these issues with Odin."

"It's okay. It isn't so bad here."

"I am glad you think so." He looked at her tiredly. "Don't train too long and lock up when you are done. I expect every single dagger returned to the correct place, not squirrelled away in your chambers."

"I will."

Loki headed back towards the library, back to his endless book repairs. Not so bad here? Well, that was a start. She definitely was not going to put those daggers away, he would have to hunt her chamber for them. He shook his head. He had plenty, but surely she could not take that many of them. He would soon discover that yes, indeed she could.

Jotunheims Queen
Chapter Nineteen
Loki's shock

Vast amounts of the upper sections of the library were repaired by the time Loki came down for dinner, grey with exhaustion. It would take another month or longer to return the library to its former glory. Even then, pieces were proving tricky to repair when it came to ancient papyrus. He would have to purchase Holly several additional books to apologise and build another wing onto the library, or two. He had need of some more poetry.

He was so tired and hungry, he did not even bother to wash or change for dinner. Taking his place at the head of the table as the sendlings laid out a rich venison stew, breads, cheese, fruit and pickles, he served himself a substantial portion, a book of poetry lay open on his lap before he realised he was no longer alone. Holly had quietly snuck into the room. He flew to his feet, regretting his grimy appearance as the fair lady stood there dressed in one of the finest vintage gowns he had created for her. The rich red velvet hung perfectly on her small frame. She looked breathtaking, he had never seen her fully dressed in the garb of his people before. She held herself in a regal way that made him even more sure she would be a fine Queen. A snap of his fingers and his own appearance changed into a lavish black suit, with a red shirt to match her. "My lady, may I be of some assistance this evening?"

"No, my lord. If you permit it, I thought I might join you for dinner."

"Of course, allow me." Loki hurried to pull out her chair, making her comfortable while the sendlings set her a place at the table, serving her stew and wine. Music started playing in the background faintly, nothing that the Midgardian would know, but certainly jolly. Candles around the room lit to give a warm, homely glow to the table. "To your health," Loki offered, lifting his goblet.

Holly echoed the words, settling them down into their first comfortable meal since the hospital. Loki glanced at the open book on the tabletop.

Would it be rude to continue reading or should he put it away? Either way it would look like he was trying to avoid the dinner and his sudden guest.

"What were you reading?" Holly asked, trying to break the stalemate.

"Some Midgardian Poetry."

"You don't seem the type for such things."

"A good poem has its moments. Would you care for me to read to you?"

"If you wish."

Once Upon a midnight dreary, while I pondered weak and weary,

Over many a quaint and curious volume of forgotten lore

While I nodded, nearly napping, suddenly there came a tapping

As if someone gently rapping, rapping at my chamber door.

"Tis some visitor" I muttered, "Tapping at my chamber door

Only this and nothing more."

Ah, distinctly I remember it was in the bleak December,

And each separate dying ember wrought its ghost upon the floor

Eagerly I wished the morrow: Vainly had I sought to borrow

From my book surcease of sorrow- sorrow for the lost Lenore

For the rare and radiant maiden whom the angels name Lenore

Nameless here for evermore

"Beautiful, dark, yet full of life," Holly commented.

Loki flicked through the pages to locate another suitable passage, eating hurried bites of his stew as he searched.

Thy soul shall find itself alone

Mid dark thoughts of the grey tombstone

Not one of all the crowd, to pry

Into thine hour of secrecy

Be silent in that solitude

Which is not loneliness For then

The spirits of the dead who stood again

In death around three, and their will

Shall overshadow thee: be still

The night though clear, shall frown

And the stars shall not look down

From their high thrones in Heaven

With light like hope to mortals given

But their red orbs, without beam

To thy weariness shall seem

As a burning and a fever

Which would cling to thee forever

"You do truly love poetry," Holly commented. "I have never known someone so passionate in their recital."

Loki shrugged. "Edgar Allan Poe, he always did write as if he saw more of the cosmos than most of your kind. Shakespeare, he was an interesting fellow. He wrote deep plays far beyond the knowledge of his era. Your Midgardian authors have talents that are not seen anywhere else in the

Nine Realms. If nothing else, that grants them reason to exist without Odin's warfare."

"You've lived a long time, did you ever meet any of them?"

Loki looked lost in thought. "Yes, yes, I did. For a number of years I lived as a travelling actor with a troop performing plays all over England. They were the happiest years I ever lived, until Odin found me and forced me back to Asgard. If I could relive any moment in my ancient existence, it would be as an actor with my troop again."

"Would you act out those plays for me one day?"

Loki sniffed, the emotion or the freely flowing wine starting to affect him. "Perhaps."

He rose from his chair holding out his hand. "Would you care to dance with me like old times?" Pleased when she accepted, he led her to the ballroom, huffing at the remains of their long-passed party. A flick of the hand and the mess was removed as he twirled her around into his arms, the scent of his favourite oils coming from her hair as she drew close. She rested her head on his chest, and in return he allowed his head to rest on hers as they danced. Another moment he wished he could remain in forever, instead of living up to his responsibilities. All too soon the night ended. They both yawned, exhausted from the day.

When Loki escorted her back to his room, he found an honest smile on his face as he prepared for bed, thinking of all the treasures he could return from Midgard with to make her smile.

■ ■

Tired but invigorated from the training session, Holly took a bath to ease her sore shoulders. Her muscles feeling like lead, she was so tired that she fell into a doze in the bathtub with the sendlings watching over her. When she woke and dried off, the first garment that caught her eye in the wardrobe was a delicate red velvet gown. It had a low neckline, but not immodest. It seemed the perfect gown for a nice evening meal. She allowed the sendlings to dress her, twisting her hair up into a curled updo to show off her collar bones. One of them brought her a jewellery box from which she chose a delicate design. A Viking compass with a pair of serpent earrings with glowing red eyes. Hiding the stolen daggers in various hiding places as she dressed, she figured the more she hid, the less likely Loki was to find and take back all of them. Although her small stature made it frustratingly difficult to use many of the best hiding spots. However, it did also open some at floor level, as she hid some in the bedframe and under the floorboards.

A few squirts of a strong yet pleasant perfume and her outfit was complete, although dressier than she was used to. She admired her princess-like appearance before heading downstairs. She no longer looked like Holly the abused teen, but she looked every inch the Ase he called her. Pausing at the doorway to the dining room, she watched Loki. His face was smeared with dirt, his clothing covered with dust. He looked exhausted to the point of collapse as he ladled stew into a bowl. He appeared too tired to even chew, his eyes semi-focused on a leather-bound book laying on the tabletop.

Feeling overdressed and like she was intruding, Holly took a step back towards the staircase to leave him to his privacy when he looked up at her. Gesturing her to the tableside, he seemed surprised that she would even design to join the table. He looked stunning in the royal clothing he had changed into, she just felt bad for bothering him when he was clearly tired. She had never seen him in dirty clothing before, he always took such pride in his appearance. He moved as if the world was on his shoulders that evening. If she had thought he would allow it, she would have moved behind his chair to massage his shoulders as he read. It was a pleasant dinner with a passionate poetry reading between courses, followed by the perfect after-dinner dancing. It was strange to be back in the place they had once danced in a lifetime ago. The familiar tune from her birthday started playing, relaxing her body into his arms as she found her head resting on his chest. She breathed in that cedar scent he always seemed to wear. She was surprised when he laid his head on hers, relaxing into the motions of the dance. He seemed so relaxed, he never allowed such vulnerability around her. The gentle swaying in his arms nearly sent her (or was it both of them?) to sleep. She found herself yawning, setting Loki off joining her. She was seeing a side of him that had been hidden to her, the real him without the dramas and lies about who he was. He seemed more relaxed in her presence now she knew the truth of his identity. Holly felt like she was learning who he was all over again.

"Let me escort you to your chambers, my lady," he offered, taking her arm and leading her upstairs. "I will leave tomorrow before you wake and I may be gone as long as a week. Any longer than that and I will make sure to send word."

They both lingered saying their goodnight well wishes, neither one wanting this beautiful night to end. Their good times together always seemed so fleeting, always ending in darkness. She hoped that tonight would not stay true to form.

The next morning, she rose early hoping to find Loki getting ready to set off, however he was long gone. The sendlings brought her breakfast and laid it out in the dining room. The library door was still stubbornly closed however many times she asked it to open, as were Loki's personal chambers. On a whim, Holly tried the back door. It opened, leading her to a courtyard where she found a well-tended herb garden next to vegetable plots. Clearly where the homestead grew its own food. Beyond that were stables and buildings for domestic animals, all tended to by the sendlings. The ground here was fertile with no snow, no ice. She could feel the magic saturating the ground. She even picked out runes marking the home in a protective manner. No wonder Loki had felt safe to leave her alone here while he travelled. This place was a fortress of spellcasting, clearly added to by an eternity of Loki's protective spells.

It became clear to her that he had never wanted to imprison her on the grounds, he had simply brought her to the most protected place that he knew of. She cursed herself for being so blind to his intentions. She had judged him so harshly, and for no need. How could she ever apologise for that? Her heart heavy, she explored further. To the walled fields surrounding the castle where she found a wooden more rustic version of an assault course, with dummies set up that looked like they were for target practice. Everything she needed to train. Well, that and a few centuries of everlasting life to play catch up to Loki's skills. She couldn't have any hope of preparing in time for this war with Odin and be any real use.

She stared at the course, putting her foot on the first balance beam. Impossible odds were not going to stop her. If she were going to die at Odin's hands, it would be under her terms not his.

■ ■

Loki crossed Midgard. It had been a long week of deals, potion selling and building allies. He needed to make sure that Holly would have protection and a safe place to go after her return. He wanted to send her back to her life as soon as he could. It just would not do to have her all locked up in the castle against her will for much longer.

The rent was paid to her slumlord, a full year in advance and far more currency in her bank account to pay any bills that might need to come out in that time, as well as a healthy amount of cash in safety deposit boxes for her living expenses when she returned. If nothing else, he wanted to make sure after all she had been through, that she could live a comfortable existence for what fleeting years she would have remained. He tried to calculate the average age of a Midgardian before death. A century or two he guessed at.

Unlocking her apartment door, he let himself into her personal space feeling the ward tickling at him as he tried to enter. She had learned his lessons well enough. Loki allowed the wards to check that he meant no ill will before entering. The apartment was tiny: a narrow corridor with sliding doors on either side to reveal a bedroom that barely housed a bed and wardrobe, on the other side a tiny shower and toilet. The corridor ended in the smallest kitchenette possible, a tiny sofa, a single bookcase and a table with only one chair. There were a handful of books on the shelf, an iPad on the table that had seen better days with a huge crack down the screen nearly breaking it in half. In the bedroom, he found a sparse collection of clothing and a tiny table with a few personal items laid there with the velvet box he had been asked to locate, resting against the books he had purchased as an apology, barely out of the wrappings from Odin attacking them soon after.

Taking the larger of her two suitcases from the top of her wardrobe, Loki packed a selection of her clothing and undergarments, half of the books, a few toiletries and the tatty old bear that lay on her pillow. If she wanted the rest, he could come back for it.

He reached out for the velvet box. It had a strange, yet familiar energy to it. It was too long and heavy to be a necklace box. He could not help but flick the box open, wondering what was inside. He had to fight back tears as he realised what she had guarded so carefully for all her life and what she wanted back so badly.

The box held the permanently frozen ice rose that he had once gifted her.

Jotunheims Queen

Chapter Twenty

Loki's Fury

Loki stormed back into the castle dropping his bags and Holly's suitcase in the great hall for the sendlings to take upstairs. "Where is she?" he demanded of the nearest shadow. The darkness indicated towards the outside. The training area, of course it would be. She needed to be strong enough to fell a God! He had thought she was telling the truth when she said she wanted to slay Odin, now Loki knew better. She was only interested in murdering Loki himself. He flew through the back door, the velvet box still in his hand. He found her dangling from a balance beam working on her upper body strength.

"Loki! Hey!" she greeted, seeing him approach. She let go, landing a little too neatly on the ground. "How was the trip?"

"What in the Nine Realms do you think you are doing?" he spat.

"The beam?" she asked, confused. "I used to be a gymnast at school and then a dancer. I did my best to stay in shape at the hospital and when I got out."

"I do not care in the slightest about your little exercises. I want to know exactly who and what you are and why you are here!" Loki demanded.

"Loki, what's going on? You know the answers to all those things. Are you okay? Did Odin hurt you?"

"Save your fake concerns for someone who cares, I do not need them."

"Lokes, tell me what is wrong, please."

"Do not use such familiar tones with me," he snapped. "I am not your 'Lokes', I am a King, **the** King of these lands! Explain yourself now before I blast you into nothingness at the roots of the Yggdrasil to die."

"Lord Loki, please tell me what you have need of being explained."

"You honestly dare to ask me that? You sent me to fetch it!"

"Fetch what?" She was exasperated.

"This!" Loki slammed the box into her hands.

"My rose!" she answered smiling, opening the box to make sure that it was undamaged by the trip. "Thank you so much for finding it."

"How do you have this? You cannot possibly have it. Bad enough that you faked being a child to astral travel to my world and build yourself a body while you were there, but now you expect me to just believe that a mere child can move matter back into the corporeal world!" Loki spat out.

Holly was confused. "You gave it to me."

"Do not play games with me. I am the God of Lies, answer me truthfully! I will know if you do not."

"Loki, I seriously do not understand why you are freaking out. You gave me this."

"I gave it to you in the astral realm," he hissed.

"Yes, and?"

"You have it in the physical world."

"So?"

"That should be impossible, unless you are an expert sorcerer and you were hiding as a mere child when I gave you this. So for the third time: How do you have this!"

Holly shrugged. "I left it in our cave for a long time. Then in the hospital, I had a lot of nightmares when I was looking for you in my dreams. I couldn't find you. Then one morning, I woke up and this was on my pillow. I thought you had left it there."

"You lie, you are manipulating me. Is this what you wanted? A chance at my throne? Access to my secrets? Is this what Odin has sent you here for? To betray me like every other woman he has sent into my life?" Loki demanded.

"Loki, you are the God of Lies as you stated. Look at me, do you think that I am lying and Odin's spy?" she asked, folding her arms and staring straight at him. She held her ground as his anger raged like a brewing storm in the courtyard. The runes hummed with the overloading power of his chaotic magic close to falling out of his control. "Loki, scan me, read me, whatever it is that you need to do and tell me if I am lying."

Loki grabbed her bare wrist, staring into her eyes for long moments before moving back, the energy dispersing. "No, you are not lying," he answered quietly.

Holly came forward, wrapping him in her arms to try and calm him. "No Loki, I am not lying. You are safe here with me."

He clung to her like she was an anchor. "Everyone betrays me in the end."

"Not me, not ever," Holly promised.

"If only I could believe that."

"I'll be here reminding you of it until you do believe it. Every single day I live."

"Why would you want to be?"

"Because you are my friend. Because I care about you."

Loki slammed her back into the castle wall. "But you shouldn't. I am nothing but a broken monster."

Holly fought back, trying to free herself. "The only monster here is Odin."

"No, I am the monster." He materialised a knife, holding it at her throat. "I should kill you now before you do."

Holly pushed back. "You wouldn't dare, you care for me too much."

"I care nothing for you! You are just a Midgardian with a limited life span that causes more problems than solutions."

"Oh really?" Holly kneed him, slamming back into him and escaping as he moved back slightly. She pulled her own knife, holding it out towards him. "Try me."

Loki knocked the knife from her hand, slamming her back into the wall. "Want to try that again, mortal?"

Holly pulled out another dagger, aiming it at his side. "Yes, I do want to try that again."

Loki laughed. "I am eternal. I have been fighting in wars beyond your comprehension since before your people even existed. Long before your realm was created. Do you think you can harm me? With no training, a handful of stolen blades, and little magic?"

"I have to try, even if you kill me for it. You are deranged. I will bring my Loki back from this monster you are acting like." She ducked away from him, using a table to give her some distance from him. She threw a dagger that missed wildly, embedding itself into the wall where she had so recently been trapped.

"A game of cat and mouse, is it?" Loki asked. "I will hunt you down and kill you. No, I will hunt you down, introduce you to my dungeons and teach you how to respect a man of my station and power."

"How very Christian Grey of you. Do I at least get to choose my own safe word?" she taunted.

"Your safe word is **dead**, which is what you will be once I am done. You came here under false pretences that you needed my aid, you abused my trust and my compassion, my lo.." Loki broke off the word, throwing the table to one side. "I will kill you, and then I will kill Odin for sending you."

"You already know me not to be a liar, you tested me. What else can I do to prove myself?" she demanded, edging back towards the training beams.

"You are a liar, you have just learned to hide it from me."

"You said that no one could lie to the Lord of Lies!"

"You clearly can, because you are lying. What you say is impossible." Loki took steps towards her.

Holly pulled herself back up onto the high beam above his head, running along it to escape. Loki set the beam on fire behind her, the blue flames chasing her. She did a flip, landing neatly on her feet before setting off into a run back into the house. She needed to find somewhere to hide until he saw sense again. "I'll keep trying as many times as it takes to knock into your stupid head that I care for you!"

"You are a honey trap, a beautiful distraction from what I should be doing, " Loki replied. He went into the kitchen looking for her, feeling with his magic for her energy.

"You think I am beautiful?" Holly asked, slamming into him and shoving him into the cool box, trying to lock him inside.

He flicked the door open with ease, turning on her. "Dark temptress, secret siren, you know what your pretty face allows you access to in men. I might be old, but I am not blind yet. Tell me why you are here!"

"I am here, because you brought me here!" She edged back away from him, looking for a fresh weapon. The only thing in reach was a cast iron frying pan, but it didn't stop her from throwing it at him.

He grabbed her, slamming her into the wall again. His hands were almost ready to tear out her throat, yet he paused. "Why couldn't you just be my Ase? Could Odin not allow me one good thing in my existence?"

"Loki, I am your Ase. I care for you a great deal. You are everything to me. It is you that do not care about me."

"I do," Loki broke off, the emotions inside of him too much to handle right now. Although one part of his body was reacting in a way that he had not expected. He pushed away, releasing her before she felt it rising. "I don't know what to think or feel anymore." He had the powerful urge to grab her face, kiss her and beg her forgiveness for his actions. What the hell was going on with him? Holly tried to put her arms around him but he pulled away. If she touched him right now, he didn't think that he would be able to prevent himself from not just kissing her, but taking her to his chambers.

"This has really shaken you. Why does it bother you so much?"

"Odin has sent others to betray me before. My second wife, Sigyn, married me and bore my children. All under Odin's orders to have me 'watched' and 'controlled.' Then there was Sif. We courted for nearly a decade. I had a ring made to propose to her on our anniversary. On that very night before I could, she publicly declared her love for an intent to marry Thor."

"No wonder you cut off her hair."

Loki chuckled. "Oh those were the days of my mischief. I was extremely drunk, high, hurt, and angry. Not a good mix for many men. The hair was her pride, I destroyed that pride like she had my heart. I wish I could trust you, Midgardian, but there is just so much I do not understand about you."

"If it helps, I don't understand much of it either." She offered her hand to him. "Can we try to figure it out together? Please? Odin is playing both of us, trying to drive us apart. We are stronger together, we always were."

"Do not betray me," Loki warned.

"Don't betray me either."

"How can we move forward from this?" he asked. He looked ready to collapse.

Holly grabbed his hand and pulled. "Let me run you a bath, you need to relax. Stop overthinking for a single evening. If Odin has a plan, it can wait until tomorrow for us to resolve it together."

For once, Loki bowed to the wishes of another person. "Thank you."

When they re-entered the castle, Loki led her towards his own suite of rooms. It would be the first time that she had ever seen it. He pushed the door open to show a dark wood panelled living area. Every surface was covered in books on magic. There was a desk buried under piles of papers and books, which were stacked up on the floor all around it, a dining table covered in maps, parchment, and various talismans and there was even a chaise longue, half covered in papers and books. He looked around sheepishly. "Sorry, I should have tidied. I receive guests so rarely in here."

Holly was already fascinated by the bookcases, wishing she had her specs with her to be able to read them. "This place is incredible. All this knowledge, all these books! I would never want to leave."

Loki smiled. "I will leave the door unlocked as long as you promise to never summon anything you cannot dispel nor blow up my castle."

"Can I accidently set fire to the castle instead?" she asked with a smirk.

"No." Loki smiled back, swatting at her with a pile of papers as he cleaned off part of the table and the chaise.

"Darn it," she muttered, leaving her rose on the table. Loki picked it up, fetching a sendling to return it to her chambers before it got lost in the sea of knowledge in his room.

"Thank you, now rest. I'll run your bath," she informed him.

"Yes, my Queen," he joked, heading into his sleeping area. A huge bed covered in furs dominated the room. There were candlesticks everywhere, cushions, pillows, a luxury place meant for…. Well, a long-time ago, it had been created for orgies lasting days on end, when he used to entertain people in his most drunken times. Between the

Ragnarök's and the betraying spouses, hehad tended to live a hedonistic lifestyle to numb the endless pain in his heart.

A smaller room led off from the sleeping area that was styled as a walk-in wardrobe full of mirrors. It housed his finest clothing for balls, galas, and special occasions, unlike the more everyday clothing that hung in his wardrobe in the main room, hidden behind the panelling. He found a robe and changed out of his travelling clothes into it. When he came out, the sunken bath was full with bubbles and candles. A bottle of mead and a single glass was placed by its side with a selection of old poetry books. It was perfect, everything he needed. He did not think that anyone had ever bothered to do anything like this in his entire life. "Ase?" he called. He reached out with his magic, she was back in the spell crafting room reading, giving him privacy to relax.

Loki lowered himself into the bath, sighing as the hot water hit all the aching places on his back. A deep glass or three of mead later, he leaned back allowing the bubbles to heal his troubles. He would have to think about why his body had reacted the way it had to her when they were fighting. But not now, now he was too far gone to make rational thoughts. The heat did nothing to ease his aching body part, yet if he touched himself to relieve the pressure, he felt sure that her face would be in his mind as he did so. Loki forced himself to close his eyes, trying to lower his heartbeat until he was calmer.

As the water cooled, it shook him awake from the deep slumber he had slipped into. Strange that he had fallen asleep when he rarely ever slept, and even rarer when it was deep sleep. He dried and redressed in sleep trousers and the robe, leaving it open slightly to show his bare clean-shaven chest. A towel was wrapped around his damp hair. How the mighty God had fallen, he looked like some heart throb from a teen movie. He found the sendlings had laid a relaxed supper of game pie, bread, cheese, and honey cakes for him, so he did not have to travel downstairs.

Holly was still busy on the other side of the castle, no doubt intentionally leaving him to eat and drink to his fill without her bothering him. A full stomach and a book later, he relaxed on the chaise. If Ase wanted to find him, no doubt she would do so. She was right however, he did need to take some time to relax. To stop overthinking what Odin's chess moves would be and to work out how he felt about Holly. And to sleep, for days if he could. It had been far too long.

Jotunheims Queen

Chapter Twenty-One

Frigg's Visitation

Holly ran him the bath, admiring the deep sunken tub which was even larger than the one in her chamber. Water poured into it, not from taps like hers, but from a natural waterfall from a hot spring that the chamber was built around. The room was designed like it was a cave, with natural rock outcroppings where she managed to wedge pieces of candle to light to make it even more magical. The space was stunning and matched its master perfectly. When she was done, she could hear Loki getting changed in his bedroom. She asked the sendlingss to bring him a light meal when he was ready, before heading to her own chambers to wash the grime from her workout away and settle into a reading session in the spell room.

She needed some time to clear her head, as horrific as their fight had been, she had to admit that being slammed into the wall hadn't been the worst thing to happen. If anything, it had been quite stimulating. She hadn't thought of her old friend that way before, but there had been a certain tell-tale dampness between her legs. Just the adrenaline? If she had feelings for Luke, or Loki, then she would have known long ago, surely? Did she honestly want to kiss him? Frustrated in more ways than one, Holly grabbed the nearest book, forcing herself to be distracted from the strange thoughts she was having. Trust her to fall for the morally grey character!

She was so deep in the book that she lost all track of time until the sendlings fetched her, tugging at her arm until she followed them down into the great hall. There was a cloaked figure in the hallway, waiting to be noticed. "You are not Loki," she commented, checking her pockets for a knife left behind by the training ready to defend herself. "Loki!" she screamed.

Loki appeared instantly behind her in his half-dressed state, also carrying knives. "Identify yourself or die where you stand."

The figure let down its black hood to show an older female figure. "Loki, you said I would be welcomed here at any time. This is not exactly welcoming."

"Lady Frigg, forgive me. This has been a long day." He made the weapons disappear., "Holly, I would like you to meet the Queen of Asgard and my old friend, Lady Frigg." He noticed her backing away, the dagger still held out. "Ase, she won't hurt you."

"You are dead," Holly hissed. "Twelve years ago, you died. I went to your funeral, I grieved for you." She slashed wildly at the person in front of her. "You can't be here, my life went to shit after you were gone."

Loki disarmed her gently. "Frigg? Can you explain? Did Odin do something I do not know about?"

"Fuck Odin, Lokes! That is my grandmother!" Holly snapped. "My dead grandmother."

"Grandmother?" Loki exclaimed. "The one that taught you about the Gods?" He had known about her, overheard some of the lessons taught when Thor had been scrying in Frigg's pool. He had never looked to see what she appeared like.

"Yes Loki, I was her grandmother, or I at least took the form of being her. I apologise for abandoning you, Lady Holly. Odin became aware of the fact I was meddling in his tasks and shielding you from his magic. If I had stayed, things would have been far worse for all of us," Frigg answered.

"Worse!" Holly spat. "After you 'died, I ended up in a mental ward where they pumped me full of drugs, used shock therapy and beat me daily, where the guards starved me, put cigarettes out on my bare skin. They kicked me, attacked me and made me live my life in fear. Where in the end, the only way I got to eat was to teach myself to pick the lock on the kitchen door. Do you have any idea at all what happened to me while you were gone? What have I suffered because of you leaving? Don't give me excuses about Odin! We three could have stood together and fought him off. But no, you were a coward!"

Holly burst into tears. Loki drew her into his arms. "Ase, beloved, you did not tell me any of that. Why did you never tell me what you went through? I would have listened, comforted you, got drunk with you. I could have been whatever you needed me to be so you could heal."

"I didn't want to be a bother," she sobbed.

"Ase," Loki said in a warning tone. "You could never be a bother to me." He kissed her hair before drying her eyes on the edge of his shirt. "Go to my room Ase, lock the door behind you. I will come up when I am done here. You will be safe, I swear it."

Holly nodded and fled up the staircase.

Frigg bowed her head to the master of the house. "Lord Loki, I did try to protect her as much as I could behind Odin's back. However, the mother complained to him about the grandmother meddling in their grand plan. If I hadn't left, he would have killed me and the child as well. I couldn't risk Holly being put to death before she was old enough to understand what was happening. She is far too important."

"Yes, she is extremely important to me. If you had bothered to come to me sooner, we might have spared her all that trauma," Loki snapped, "Look at her, she lost ten years of her pitifully short life. Ten years she should have been living her life, loving, learning."

"I wish things could have been different. I never wanted to cause either of you pain."

Loki took a deep breath trying to stop himself from lashing out at her. "You brought her the rose from the astral realm?" he asked.

"She needed a reason to hold on."

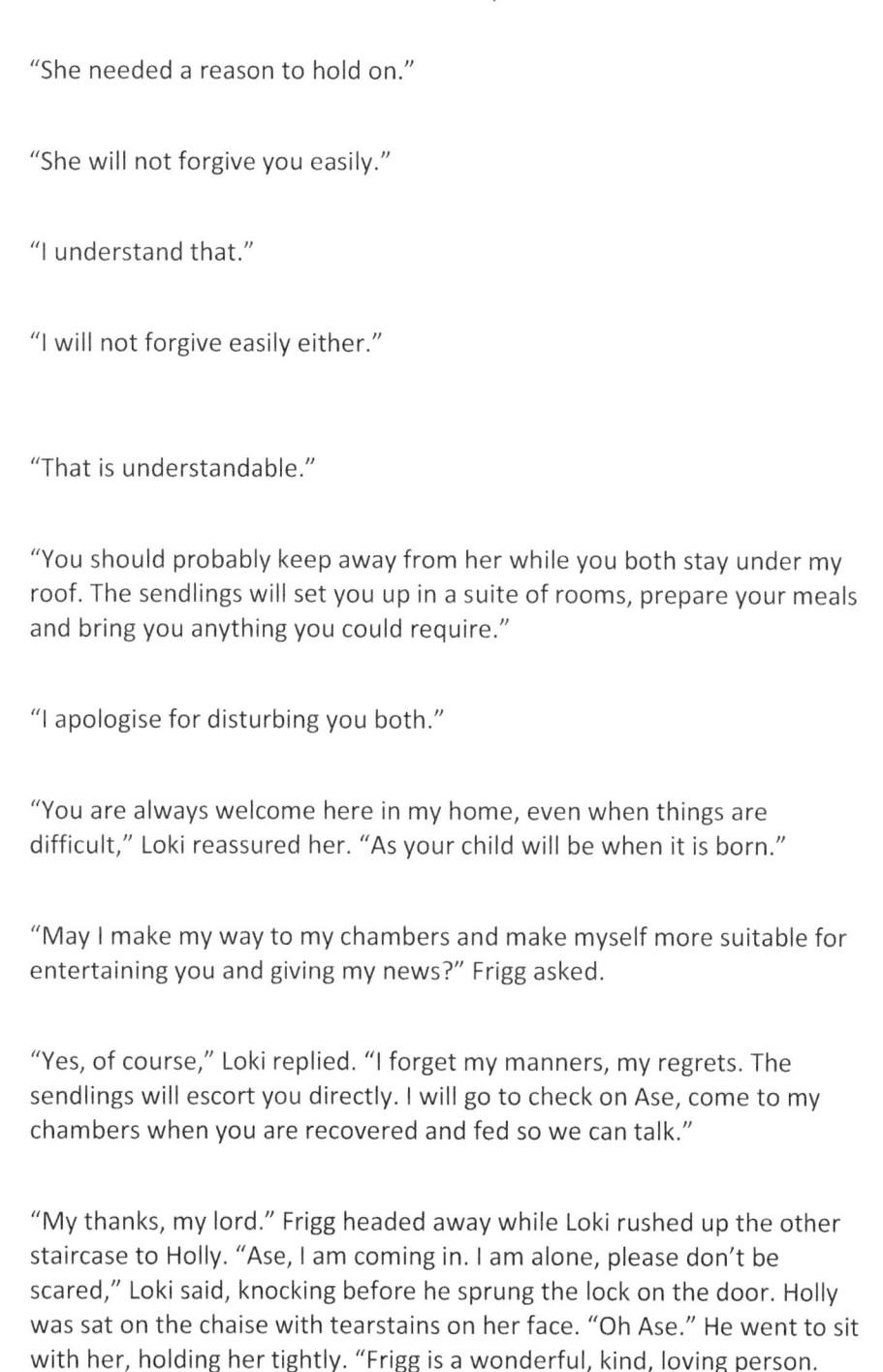

"She will not forgive you easily."

"I understand that."

"I will not forgive easily either."

"That is understandable."

"You should probably keep away from her while you both stay under my roof. The sendlings will set you up in a suite of rooms, prepare your meals and bring you anything you could require."

"I apologise for disturbing you both."

"You are always welcome here in my home, even when things are difficult," Loki reassured her. "As your child will be when it is born."

"May I make my way to my chambers and make myself more suitable for entertaining you and giving my news?" Frigg asked.

"Yes, of course," Loki replied. "I forget my manners, my regrets. The sendlings will escort you directly. I will go to check on Ase, come to my chambers when you are recovered and fed so we can talk."

"My thanks, my lord." Frigg headed away while Loki rushed up the other staircase to Holly. "Ase, I am coming in. I am alone, please don't be scared," Loki said, knocking before he sprung the lock on the door. Holly was sat on the chaise with tearstains on her face. "Oh Ase." He went to sit with her, holding her tightly. "Frigg is a wonderful, kind, loving person.

She would never intentionally cause you pain. She just did what she thought was best, even if it was foolish."

"I wish she had never left," Holly sobbed.

"I know, I wish she could have stayed as well. I wish that I could have." Loki held her, allowing her to cry it out.

"Is there anything I can fetch for you? Anything that you need? What would help you to feel better?"

"Can you just hold me for a while, is that okay?" she asked.

A strange request, but one he was more than happy to reward. "Always. Relax, I will stay as long as you need me to." They sat cuddled up in silence, Loki listening as her breath mellowed out and she fell asleep. Not wanting to disturb her rest, Loki picked up his book to start reading again.

It was many a year ago

In a kingdom by the sea

That a maiden there lived

Whom you may know

By the name of Annabel Lee

And this maiden she lived

With no other thought

Than to love and be loved by me

By the Norns, what was he doing reading love poems? He admonished himself. He knew better than to fall in love with anyone after the amount of times he had been betrayed. Yet, cuddled up like he was with Holly, he hadn't been this happy in a long time. Could the others be correct, was he falling in love with a Midgardian?

Holly stirred in his arms. "What are you reading?"

Was he dreaming or had she just pressed her lips to his bare chest? He held out the book so she could see. "I thought you were sleeping."

"I don't sleep that much, I mostly have bad dreams." She flicked through the pages. "More poetry, Loki?"

"I told you before, I enjoy the writing," Loki huffed, snatching back his book.

"Who would think that the God of Mischief has a soft side?" she teased.

"Do you want me to dump your behind on the floor or do you want cuddles?" Loki commented.

"Cuddles," she answered, squeezing closer.

"Then hush and let me read to you."

"Sorry Luke."

"Shh, I said."

I was a child and she was a child

In this kingdom by the sea

But we loved with a love that was more than love

I and my Annabel Lee

With a love that the winged seraphs of Heaven

Coveted her and me

Sometime later a soft knock came at the door. Loki moved his hand lazily to open it with his magic, too relaxed and sleepy to move. Frigg took in the scene in front of her, the two curled up on the sofa together covered in furs and Loki reading aloud. It looked so romantic that she was sad she had intruded. "My regrets for the disturbance, you said to attend when I had rested."

Loki looked up, the tiredness not leaving his eyes. "That is not an issue, please, come in." He touched Holly's head with a sleep rune to prevent her from being woken by their talking. Sneaking out from under the furs, he didn't realise he was still only half dressed. "Would you care for a drink?" he offered, pouring them both a glass of mead.

"Only one," Frigg answered, touching her growing bump.

"May I?" he asked, waiting for permission before touching the baby bump. "Your son is growing strong, he will make you a good heir."

"Thank you." They sat at the dining table, Frigg glancing over at the sleeping Midgardian. "You have great affection for that one," she commented.

Loki couldn't help smiling when he looked over at her as well. "I do, she is a good friend."

"Just a friend?"

"Why does everyone keep asking that?" Loki demanded. "First Thor, now you." Not to mention his own body's thoughts.

"Perhaps we see what you are still blind to."

"I knew her as a child," Loki snapped. "I saw her grow up. It would be disgusting to feel that kind of affection for her." He went to rise from the table.

Frigg held up her hand. "I meant no disrespect in your house."

"I can't possibly have those kinds of feelings, not for her."

"Loki, is she still a child?"

"No."

"Did you feel romantically towards her as a child?"

Loki looked like he would be ill. "Of course not. I would never do that to a child. I am a father, a good father. I would never allow anyone to touch an underage person in my presence, I would slaughter them."

"So, when did you start to feel romantically towards Holly?"

"How many times must I say I do not have those kinds of feelings?"

"You used to be a much better liar, lie smith."

Loki looked embarrassed. "A few weeks ago, soon after she had to be brought here for safety. There is just something about her. So fresh, so different. She stands up to me. Tells me no, shouts at me when she feels I am wrong. No one dares to do that. She is insane, has no concern for her own safety. It drives me to distraction worrying that she is going to get herself killed and I won't be able to get there in time. She is even teaching herself to fight so she can join us in this war. Not a single thought to the fact she is mortal, and we all are not. She will be the death of me!"

"Or the making of you."

"It is so strange, the more I spend time with her, the more it feels like I know her, like I have always known her."

"You should focus on that more, when you have the time."

"What do you mean by that?" he asked.

"I mean that Odin may have hexed you as much as he has Holly."

"Explain yourself," Loki demanded.

"I cannot, my tongue is literally tied with a spell."

"Did I know Holly before this mortal life of hers?" Loki demanded.

Frigg folded her hands on the tabletop. "I am not permitted to answer that for you, under Odin's orders."

"Frigg!" Loki snapped, ready to pursue this subject more when he was distracted by an explosion in the far distance, he leapt to his feet. "Wake the girl and get your armour on. Odin has come."

Chapter Twenty-Two

Odin's Warning

Moments later, Loki was in the armoury wrapping daggers around every part of his body, mentally counting how many were missing that he would have to steal back from her chambers. One nice night, which was all he had desired with his Ase and how many interruptions now?! All these years of planning and Odin just had to pick tonight to make his first move! Loki was overtired, mildly drunk and emotionally wrung out. Not at his best for fighting. He wanted to strangle Odin with his bare hands for taking away something so precious.

Frigg made her way into the armoury, armour double strapped around her stomach, protecting the unborn child. A sword hung at her waist. "This is a decoy Loki, he is only testing you. He won't have done much harm, not yet."

"I am aware however, I must check on my people. Prepare for our return movements and clear up any issues with my warriors. The most important things are to keep you, your baby and Ase safe." He laid his hand on her belly, blue magic coming from his fingertips laying powerful protection on them both.

Holly stumbled into the room dressed in trousers, a loose shirt and still attempting to tie up the straps on the leather armour that he was not even sure how she had found in her size. "What's going on Lokes?" She paused to admire him in his armour, sure the tease of a clean-shaven chest under his open shirt had been stunning, but somehow the armour made him look even more attractive.

"Holly, what are you wearing and why are you here?" He was annoyed, the sendlingss had to have helped her, the sendlings that were meant to follow his commands, not hers.

"I'm going with you." She started raiding the left-over daggers that he hadn't strapped onto his own body yet, abandoning tying up the armour as she couldn't get the straps right.

"Stop stealing my daggers every chance that you get," Loki hissed, grabbing one back. "You are not going with us, you are staying here where it is safe."

Holly stared him out. "No, I am not. I am going with you." She grabbed the dagger back again.

"I said you are staying here, do as you are told woman!"

"If you want something to sit and stay when you tell it to, buy a dog." She squared up to him. "I am going with you, even if you lock me up in the castle. I will escape and follow you anyway."

"My wards will keep you in place, where you are safe. Do you understand the word safe? It means not torn to shreds by Odin's army because you are mortal."

"Do you honestly think that with a library of unlimited knowledge, I haven't found at least a dozen ways around your wards by now?" she countered.

"You are bluffing."

"Try me."

"You will get yourself killed."

"Like you don't risk the exact same thing. You ask me to be this grand figurehead of a Queen but still, you expect to lock me in your tower like I am Rapunzel. No! If you want me to be your Queen, let me act like I am one. Yes I have to learn, but I utterly refuse to just sit here and wait to see if you come back from war or not like some military spouse. So, let me come with you or watch me follow behind because I am not staying here alone," she insisted.

Loki looked at the little firecracker in front of him. He had never in his existence ever wanted to kiss someone as much as he did currently. As if admitting he had feelings had somehow made it impossible to hide them from himself anymore. He cursed Odin again for choosing tonight to attack when he could be exploring his feelings with her in his cavernous bed. "Fine, but don't expect me to mourn when you end up getting yourself killed. Which you no doubt will," he snapped back. "I will purchase you your own set of daggers next time I leave the realm as you seem to have a strong obsession for stealing mine." He grabbed the armour, snapping the laces into place with years of practice. "Fetch your cloak and some good boots before I change my mind."

Frigg smiled to herself at their interactions.

"Not one word, not even one I swear it," Loki warned.

"I would not dream of it," she promised, laughing.

"Uh huh, I can sense your judgement."

"What could I possibly be judging if you feel nothing for her?" Frigg countered.

"Just be silent!" Loki retorted with none of his usual vocal flair, just proving further just how much this conversation was getting under his skin.

Holly joined them in the great hall ready to fight. Loki checked over her armour one last time before tying her cloak over the top. "Stay behind us, if I tell you to run, you do it. Or I will blast you straight back to this castle. I do not know how dangerous it will be out there."

"I understand," Holly answered. She allowed him to win this one verbal battle. She had to concede he knew much more about battle than she did at this point.

"Good," Loki snapped. "Ladies, if you would care to step through my portal." He opened the castle door into the wild snowstorm and mountains in the background which were peppered with the odd snow-covered tree for shelter. "Watch yourselves."

They stepped through into the wilderness of Jotunheim. Loki looked around them, holding his hand up to make them pause. He could feel dark magic all around them. A horrible itchy feeling crept down his spine. Odin had been here, not so long ago, but for now he was gone. Loki couldn't see what had been done by the magic, nor trace it to anywhere. It was just lingering in the air like a nauseating smell which made him even more concerned. "Watch where you step, stay in my footprints," he warned.

The procession slowly made their way into the mountains, watching every step for traps, tricks or attacks. It almost felt like an anti-climax when they got to the entrance to the cave system safely. Loki felt around again, desperately looking for what the danger was so he didn't bring any to his people. Still the most he could see was a few crushed trees, and the odd crater like something had been fired into the snow. This was bad. If Odin was being sneaky, they had no hope.

Frustrated, Loki opened the cave, letting them down into the bowels of the realm. Down deep staircases into the dark depths that no Midgardian had ever seen. Just a handful of torches lit their way. At the base of the staircase, they entered a large open chamber set with chairs and a large table.

"This looks very King Arthur and the Knights of the Round Table," Holly commented.

Loki shushed her. "My lady Angroboda, may we please have your permission for an audience. We know that Odin has started the war. It is time to end it, on our own terms."

A tall woman dressed in furs and armour came into view. "My Lord Loki, how good of you to come at our time of need." She gracefully joined the table, clapping her hands for servants to bring and pour wine. "My Lady Frigg, you are most welcome at our table. Are you here to speak for Odin?"

"My Lady, I no longer speak for Odin. I am a free woman and speak only for myself. I do not agree with his actions towards your people. I cannot stand by while innocent people are coming to harm for no good reason. I offer my services and that of my Valkyries to your war. My son Thor, he also pledges his armies to your efforts."

"The Lady Frigg of Jotunheim, you are even more welcome at this table." Angroboda's eyes flickered to Holly. "Midgardian, why are you here? This battle is nothing to do with you or your people."

Holly looked to Loki for permission before she spoke. When he nodded, she moved forward. "My Lady, I may be of Midgard, however I disagree that this is not my fight. Odin has targeted me since childhood, attacking me constantly. Loki is my friend, I care about him and this realm. I have limited skills but if you have me, I will lend what I have to aid your people."

"Is this your Ase?" Angroboda asked of Loki.

"Yes, this is she." He put an arm around her waist protectively.

"So, you are the Midgardian that started this war?"

"I am?" Holly glanced at Loki. "Did I start all of this?"

Angroboda laughed bitterly. "You did not tell the Midgardian the story of your visit to Asgard and screaming at Odin to leave your Ase alone or you would go to war against him? Two realms linked in this battle for the sake of one girl."

"No, I told her only what she needed to know. She had enough to deal with," Loki answered.

"What is this girl to you, Loki? A consort? A lover? A pet? A slave? What makes this one girl worth war?"

"She is my friend, and in time and with training, she will be my Queen."

"A consort then," Angroboda commented.

"No!" Loki thundered, his voice filling the room. "I will not defend my relationship with this woman ever again. Nothing about our relationship is based upon a sexual nature. Ase is a bridge between our realm and Midgard. She is caring, honest and true. She will be an asset to our people. An alliance with Midgard would be a start to Jotunheim becoming aligned with all the Nine Realms as well as a worthy rival to the might of Asgard."

Angroboda looked the Midgardian up and down. "She will do," she answered scathingly. She turned and swept herself away. "Your chambers are all waiting, we will speak at morning light."

"Yes, we will," Loki answered coldly, allowing the servants to lead them away.

"Who is she?" Holly asked.

"Angroboda, my regent. I leave her to rule while I travel the realms as I have need to. She is the mother to three of my children."

Holly pouted her lips as they walked. "Your wife then."

"Ex-wife," Loki answered. "We had our time, but that was long ago. We are better as co-ruling council of our people than we are in a marriage bed. She has a new wife now I believe, they seemed extremely happy together at my last visitation."

"You could have warned me about all of this, and you should have told me it was all my fault you were at war," Holly demanded. "Not just bringing me here and dropping a wife and everything else on me."

"And what good would that have done?" Loki asked. "To tell you that I went to war for you? A child being bullied by Odin, just like he had my own blood children. I had enough of his boorish, arrogant, abusive way of rule. Sometimes you need to understand that I do what I do for your own good!"

Holly glared at him. "I am not a child anymore, stop treating me as one!"

"Then learn to act like a Queen and a warrior instead of a brat. You have no place in this war. At first light, I will escort you back to the castle and lock you where you can bring no harm to yourself or others," Loki snapped.

"What was the point of dragging me out here just to have me judged by someone you claim is your ex and then send me back home? You agreed to allow me to fight, so let me."

"No Holly, you have no place here or anywhere in my life," Loki answered.

"You disgust me. You really are a monster. A beast." She slammed into the room that the servant had brought her to, leaving Frigg and Loki behind.

"Too far Loki, far too far," Frigg commented, allowing herself entry to her own chamber to rest.

Loki stood breathing heavily at Holly's door thinking about knocking and apologising, but he couldn't quite make himself do it. He turned, entering his own chamber. It was better if she was out of harm's way, she was just a mortal. He couldn't bear it if anything happened to her. He would just have to try to repair the friendship when the war was over.

Lucinda Greyhaven

Chapter Twenty-Three

A Secret Ability

Loki lay on the bed in his temporary chamber staring at the ceiling. There was no hope of sleep. He knew he was to blame for Holly's pain. He was taking out his confused feelings on her, something she neither deserved nor was good for her. She was only semi trained in magic and barely becoming passable with a dagger. All these weeks locked up in the castle together and not once had he bothered to train her or prepare her for this war in any way. If she died, he would only have himself to blame.

Feeling guilty, Loki found his way into the communal area where he found some of the Jotuns cooking. They were more than happy to spare their King a satisfying meal and a few bottles of the home brew, one that was strong enough to even knock him on his ass. To help him forget the intense pain he had inflicted on others. Of course, it would be far easier to just knock on her door, apologise and kiss her like he was longing to, but Loki never did anything the uncomplicated way. Or even the right way most of the time. He sat there watching people milling around, finishing drinks, starting to head to their bedchambers for the night. It was strange to be around so many people. He had lived too long in isolation.

"Loki, do you ever do anything other than drink?" Thor asked him, taking a seat at his side.

Loki rolled his eyes. "I only drink when the day ends in a 'y'."

"What did you do this time? You look about fifteen minutes away from passing out. You only ever drink that heavily when you are in the most intense of pain."

"How about, hello Loki, hello Thor, what brings you to Jotunheim this fine evening?"

"Loki, you know why I am here."

"No, I do not. The last we spoke you stated that you would be neutral and remove your army from the field of play. Then, I hear from Frigg that you are coming here to fight for us, not Odin. Which makes me wonder what changed?" Loki asked.

"That is a story for another day, however my sword and my armies' swords are at your disposal. Is that not enough for you?" Thor asked.

"I would rather know the motives of my foot soldiers before I go into battle with them. Saves being turned on mid battle. If you are going to betray me, just tell me now so I can stab you in the midst of it all, saving us both the trouble," Loki answered, drinking more heavily from the bottle.

"Stop deflecting, and tell me what is hurting you so deeply tonight that you are in such a state?"

Loki took another long swig from the bottle before Thor grabbed it from his drunken fingers. "Hey!"

"Enough Loki, tell me what is wrong."

"I did something foolhardy."

"Which was?"

"I fell in love."

"Oh Loki."

"Don't 'Oh Loki' me, it was a mistake. Putting us both in danger. You know what Odin does to my loved ones."

"Does she feel the same?"

"I might be a fool, but you think me so utterly foolhardy as to tell her right before we go to war together? No, better she does not know and does not have to spurn my advances awkwardly." Loki stood, swaying heavily, starting to regret a lot more than his emotional state that night.

"Loki, take it slowly. You have drunk enough to fell a Jotun three times your size."

"I am perfectly fine," Loki retorted, which might have fooled Thor if he hadn't had to grab a bowl hurriedly to be sick into.

"Loki, you do need to find a way to express your emotions without the hangovers," Thor warned, helping the taller man to his feet and to his chamber. Stopping once when he thought he heard footsteps behind them. Seeing no one, he continued to the chamber helping the barely aware giant into the bed. "Sleep it off, and tomorrow, tell Holly how you feel before it is too late!"

Holly fumed in her room for hours. She did not fit in this world, Loki had made that perfectly clear. All this war was because of her, therefore if Odin got what he wanted, he might stop hurting innocent people. It had to be worth a try. She had no living family, no lover and only one person she had thought of as a friend until tonight. It did not matter if Odin killed her, there would be no one to miss her and certainly, she no longer cared if she lived or not.

She waited until the corridor was quiet before sneaking out. She paused at the end of the row hearing Loki and Thor deep in conversation. Loki was drunk (as usual), barely able to stand. The worst state she had ever seen him drink himself into. It looked like Thor was about to drag him to bed to sober up. She needed to be fast. Holly ducked into a nook in the stonework, putting up a weak glamour spell she hoped would be enough to hide her as they passed by.

As soon as they were out of sight, Holly made her way up the staircase. Creeping up, trying not to make a sound, the torches lit at her every step. What she hadn't considered was the fact the opening would only open by magic and her magic just wasn't cutting it. Too ashamed to return to her room, Holly bedded down near the door, hidden by a rock outcropping.

Her persistence paid off when around dawn she was woken by a hunting party heading out onto the ice plains. She snuck out behind them, unsure of which way to go. Somewhere Odin could find her without harming anyone else. She was not even sure which way the castle lay from where she was now, or even the cave of her youth. Holly took a gamble, cutting along the mountain line away from the hunting party moving as quietly as she could, away from where any of the Jotuns could find her.

Holly's plan would fall apart if Loki found her before she could find Odin. Although drinking as heavy as he had, she should have a few more hours until he was awake or aware. It might have been just minutes or long hours before she found her way to a large open ice plain with the snow hammering down on her cold body. This was where she could try to connect with the Gods she needed to.

"Okay, if I have my mythology right Heimdall, you should be able to both see and hear me. Your eyes see everything, so here I am. Alone, undefended and wishing to broker peace with Odin," she stated, her voice quivering with the cold. The cold, not fear she told herself. "Odin, you asshole. If you want me so badly, then take me. Stop this war, stop hurting people on my account. You want to destroy someone, here I am, do it. No one else, just me. Kill me and end your stupidity with Loki and his people. End this war."

No response.

"Stop taking your anger out on Loki and his family. Loki does not deserve your hatred. I have no idea why you hate us both, but just do it. Kill me and then everyone else can try to heal from this nightmare. One Midgardian is not worth all of this! This whole thing is just so stupid!"

"Midgardian." Odin appeared behind her.

She looked around to check they were alone. "Shouldn't there have been a crack of thunder or a rainbow bridge or something?"

"Whatever makes you think we left Jotunheim?" Odin asked. "Grab her." Odin's spell disintegrated, showing a full battalion of Asgardian warriors, armed and ready to attack.

"Why do you hate me so much? What did a child ever do to you?" Holly demanded.

"You were born, child, which was enough. You might not yet know what you will become. I do and I will stop that at any cost for the sake of Asgard," Odin oared.

"For Asgard!"

The warriors attacked, but Holly ran. There wasn't anywhere for her to go, she couldn't possibly make it back to the line of the mountains in time to try and hide. There were just too many of them. Her magic was limited to just a handful of tricks. She used them to raise up the snow, pelting the guards with it. A trick she had learned to try to beat Loki in a snow fight. The snow barely slowed them down, so she kept on running, dodging swords and knocking people back with the snow. It was just her buying time, moment by moment until she could think of something else.

She saw the ancient bone sticking out of the snow, revealed by her snow movements. Now she knew exactly what she had to do. Holly finally had hope of escaping this.

■■■

Loki woke up to both a pounding in his head and on his chamber door. He cursed his weakness from the night before as he stumbled towards the door, hair half out of its usual braids, springing out all over the place, his clothing rumpled. "Frigg, it is far too early. Let me sleep."

Frigg slapped him. "It is time that you stopped wallowing in self-pity and became a man. Holly is gone, she left you this!" She slammed a piece of paper into his chest, looking like she wanted to stab him in the chest instead.

Loki dumbly opened the paper, staring woozily at the page until the words mostly came into focus:

Loki, forgive me please for ruining your life and for causing this pointless war. I do not want anyone to be hurt because of me or even worse, dying for me. No, you are right. I do not fit in your world, and it seems like I may never do so. It is time I went to Odin and ended this. I will offer my life in exchange for your people's freedom. Please, do not follow me. Let me make this sacrifice. It is better for everyone involved if it ends this way. I will care for you until my dying breath. Your Ase.

Loki stared at the page, feeling tears prickle at his eyes. "She is gone?"

"In the night it seems and she snuck out with the early hunting parties to get around the magic seal. She is clever, I give her that," Frigg answered.

"She is gone," Loki repeated to himself. The words started to sink into his still heavily drunken mind. "I have to find her." He rushed out the room towards the staircase.

"Loki, wait. You can't go alone, or looking like that!" Frigg shouted. "Thor, hurry! He is going after her."

Loki did not stop, did not even care about his dishevelled appearance. All he could think of was getting to his Ase before it was too late. On the surface, he knelt on the snow trying to discern the footsteps of the Jotuns from Thor and his army, to locate her smaller feet. He was so entranced in his work, he didn't hear Frigg, Thor and Angroboda fall into step behind him.

"He truly does love this mortal," Angroboda commented to Frigg, seeing his state of appearance.

"Yes, he does. He just lacks the ability to put that into words to tell her," Frigg responded.

"It has been plain to see for everyone but him for some time," Thor added.

"I do not think Holly has worked out his feelings yet. If she had, perhaps she would not have run off to make the sacrifice in the first place," Frigg commented.

"I think it shows the depths of her feelings for this damn fool that she has," Angroboda stated.

Loki (still oblivious) to those around him, kept tracking the footsteps. He was concerned as soon as he realised which direction she had chosen. She was heading towards the site of the original Jotun/Asgardian war where thousands of his kind had been slaughtered. A sombre place that he had tried to avoid, the ghosts of the past still laid heavy on the lands. With his ties to the Underworld through his daughter (Hel), he was a little too sensitive to the spirits of the fallen warriors. Magic flew near and he felt both Odin's and Holly's.

He sped up, trying to follow the feeling of the magic. When Holly came into view and she was still alive, he couldn't even begin to describe his emotions. Not only was she alive, but she was also fighting back against a God! Using the childish tricks that he had taught to her as if they were a weapon and frankly, it was working. It was nothing Odin's army had ever seen before. She was holding back a small army of Odin's best. It would not last for long, but it was telling of how much her study was paying off that she was holding her own alone at all.

Loki saw her fall back, knocked by one of the soldiers, gaining a deep gash on her upper arm that would sting to high Hel when she realised it was there. He called forth his own blue magic fire, ready to join her when he was blasted back into the snow on his ass as a huge wave of death magic hit. Ase shouldn't know any death magic, they had never reached necromancy in their studies. He would have brought Hel in to teach those lessons as she had far more experience than he did. Loki dragged himself back onto his feet, watching Ase as she was surrounded by dozens of spectral frost giants attacking Odin's warriors, forcing them back. One of the warriors fell to a frost giant's blade, only to be reborn as one of them. He was vaguely aware of the other three coming to join him.

"When did you teach her necromancy?" Frigg asked.

"I did not, she never showed any interest in that side of magic. She actively avoided such things in all the spell books I gave her," Loki answered.

Angroboda clapped him on the shoulder. "We have our secret weapon. If she can raise every fallen warrior in this grove, we will have more than enough of an army to defend ourselves."

"I had no idea she could do this," Loki muttered. "How can she be doing this!"

Holly in the distance, fighting off the army alone before Odin called down the Bifrost, taking them all back to Asgard before they had any more casualties. She looked exhausted, ready to drop. Loki was at her side in a split second, holding her up, healing her arm before she knew she was being watched. "When did you learn necromancy? Who taught you?" Loki asked.

"I could always do it, no one ever taught me. It was just there. I didn't even know they were ghosts at first. That is why my mother called me evil. I could see, talk to and pass over spirits. I never tried raising any until today," she answered.

"How did you even begin to raise the dead with no training?" he asked. "You should be dead. That is serious heavy duty magic my daughter would struggle with on mass, and she is the Queen of Helheim."

Holly looked at him as if he had asked something stupid. "I asked them to help me."

"You just sensed the dead and asked them to help you?" Loki exclaimed.

"Why, how would you do it?" she replied. "Was I wrong?"

Loki shook his head. "I have no words for you, my little Ase. I truly do not, you have turned my silver tongue to lead. Stolen the words of the words smith. Come, let us get you warm, fed and below ground to rest."

"No!" Holly fought her way out of his arms. "I am not putting anyone else at risk. And I am not going back to the castle like a child locked away from the world. I would rather die."

"Ase, I can assure you that you have proven here that you are no child. I regret my harmful words and hope in time, that you can find it in yourself to forgive them and me."

"You made me feel stupid, like a burden," Holly snapped defensively.

"I regret that more deeply than you can imagine. I am sorry, my Ase."

"You look like hell."

Loki laughed, pulling her back into his arms. "Yes, I do, and you do not look much better. Please, will you come back with me?"

"Not just back. Will you raise your army of the dead again and fight with us when Odin returns? You are the worthy Queen of Jotunheim, Midgardian or not," Angroboda asked.

"All I want to do is fight at Loki's side for his people, for our people," Holly answered.

"Come back with us, please," Frigg asked. "We can talk when you are rested, both of you."

"Lady Ase, I pledge my army to you as well. I am Thor, Son of Odin. I apologise for my father's deeds and ill actions towards you." He bowed low and gracefully.

Holly, exhausted and overwhelmed agreed, letting them lead her back to the camp not thinking to question just how overprotective and clingy Loki was being as they headed back to safety.

Lucinda Greyhaven

Chapter Twenty-Four

Something There That….

(Or Loki finally admits his feelings)

When they got back underground, Loki excused himself which left Frigg to find Holly a hot meal and send her off to bed. Holly thought she heard crying from Loki's room as she passed by it but discounted it as a foolish idea that he would be doing that. What could Loki be crying over? She didn't think she had seen him properly cry since the night they had said goodbye at the hospital and even then, no doubt it was only because he had wasted so many years training an apprentice only to end up having to start again with someone new.

With that bitter thought in her heart, Holly slept fitfully, waking as the sun set. Washing and dressing in a fresh set of warrior clothing, she headed out to find Loki. Pausing by his door, she saw him halfway to drinking himself stupid all over again. "You have quite the drinking problem," she commented, coming to sit by him.

Loki glared at her. "For your information, I have no problems at all with drinking alcohol. I find it most therapeutic. It is everyone and everything else that I have a problem with and their incessant need to get in the way of me drinking it."

"You need help."

"I need another bottle, leave me in peace," Loki fumed, sipping at the dregs of his bottle while he felt around to see if he had another one to quench the darkness in his soul. He visibly relaxed when he found a suitable replacement bottle. Drinking deeply, more deeply than he should, he tried to ignore the Midgardian's gaze. He took a seat by the fireside in his room, stoking the flames higher as he worked his way towards oblivion.

Jotunheims Queen

Holly moved to sit with him again, warming her hands on the flames and playing a little game of trying to move them higher with her magic. "Do people realise?" she asked vaguely.

"Do people realise what?" He asked between gulps of the home brew.

"That you only drink to self-medicate your PTSD? All your tricks, the games that you play, are a clown-like persona that you carry around everywhere to cover the broken wounds of your tattered heart."

"I am a soldier, a warrior, a tactician, it is my duty to my realm and my people to protect them from attack."

"Yes, it is. That does not stop your duty from being traumatic. Nor does it negate all that Odin took from you or put you through," Holly said gently. "You went through too much too often to be any form of okay, hence the clown act you are putting on. Do you at least have someone to talk to about this weight crushing your shoulders and your life?"

"No," Loki said quietly, his voice rough from emotion. He offered the bottle to his friend.

Holly took it, taking a long swig before offering it back. "I am worried about you Loki."

"Why would you be?" Loki asked gruffly. "I have done nothing to warrant it, I have done nothing but put you in harm's way. Hurt you since you were a child." He paused in his drinking to brush a stray hair from her face, fighting the overwhelming urge to kiss her as it struck him again. "And yet, my little Ase, you see me better than anyone ever has for my entire existence. Better than any of my own spouses ever did. It is like we have known each other for eternities." He sighed, trying to find the words in his drunken mind to express what his heart was trying to say. "Ase, I am a broken creature. Being a God and a King does not hide the truth, there is little left inside of me. I am nothing more than this bottle and my pain."

"I know Loki, I knew that the first time that I met you. I could sense that you were lonely. I was too. Perhaps two lonely and broken people can find a way not to be lonely together?" Holly suggested. "Seriously, what have you got to lose? If everything goes to hell, you still have your bottle to sink into."

"Why would you want to do that for me? I am not worth your efforts," he asked.

"Because I care about you."

He couldn't stand it any longer, the tension between them. The drink had lowered his boundaries, it was screaming at him to shut the fuck up and just make a damned move already! Could she spurn him? No doubt she could, but in that second, he didn't care. He just knew that if he didn't act now, he would burst from the sheer effort of hiding what he felt any longer. Loki leaned forward, pulling her into a kiss. Slow, tender, full of an insecure need to be finally loved. A rising hope that she could be his Queen in every sense of the word, not just a figurehead of the nation. He wanted her to love him back as deeply as he was falling for her. He put everything he couldn't say into that kiss, everything his heart wanted to tell her.

When they broke apart for air, Holly smiled at him, stroking his face. "Where did that come from?"

"I wanted to," he answered, stumbling for words. "I think, Ase, Holly. I have loved you since I saw you cross the street to go to work. I cannot imagine a single day of my life without you. Living with you in the castle, I wanted to drag you to my bed every night. Even more so when we were fighting." He broke off to kiss her again, losing himself in the feel of her against him. "Oh, my beloved, you have no idea how close you were to me making love to you when you pushed me against the wall before, sparring with me. I needed you, I still do. You are the only thing in my life that makes sense. You are everything to me. The sun, the moon." He cursed under his breath. "It is so much easier when I am reading you poetry to express my feelings."

Holly pulled him into a third kiss, exploring his mouth. She wanted more of him, so much more. "Loki, you should have taken me in the weapons room. I wanted you, more than I can say. I love you. I think I have since the diner. You are my life."

"You love me?"

"Yes, I love you. My Loki, my God."

Loki groaned as she climbed into his lap, kissing down his neck. "Ase," he hissed. "I am drunk, horny and very much in love with you. I have extraordinarily little control and it grows lesser by the second."

Holly stopped long enough to stare him in the eyes and say two remarkably simple words. "Fuck control."

"Ase!" he hissed, as she claimed his mouth with her own. He pulled her closer, breathing in every inch of that perfume he loved so much. His head was swimming, all he could think of was taking her to his bed and making love to her for hours, yet he still tried to stop himself. To be sure that she knew what was happening with no regrets. He pulled back from the kisses, willing his cock to enjoy itself a little less. "Holly, my love, if you kiss me even once more, I do not think I can stop. You are intoxicating."

"Loki, make love to me. I need you inside of me. Show me what a God can do," she begged. "We have both waited far too long, please. Let us have tonight."

Loki growled, begging was his one deepest weakness. "Then come to bed my Queen, make your King proud." He picked her up in his arms, taking her to the bed. Laying her down gently, his magic had removed both of their clothing before they even touched the mattress. Her body set his aflame as they kissed. "Ase," he moaned as she ran her nails down his back.

"Loki, my Loki, only mine."

"Yours," he hissed, finding a spot on her neck that tasted better than anything he had tasted in his entire life. "Damn it Ase, you drive the beast in me to the surface!"

"I am not scared of it, give me you. The real you, in all its glory."

Loki slammed her back onto the mattress, holding her in place as his rough kisses traced down her body. He had never realised how beautiful she was, how amazing her body was. He was already aching to be inside of her. The rough moans as he teased her nipples, hardening him to a state he hadn't known was possible. His hand dipped between her legs, softly rimmed with short hair. He preferred that to the clean-shaven phase Midgard seemed to adore. She wasn't just damp, she was soaking wet. As desperate for his touch as he was for hers. It wasn't enough, even as she groaned under his fingers as he teased her. He needed more, he needed everything that she could give.

His kisses worked their way lower, taking their time around her side which drove her even more crazy as he found a spot that was sensitive to the touch. Was sex meant to be like this? Deep and meaningful? Instead of a quick roll and then shower, before moving to the next person he needed to ally with. His cock rubbed against the sheet, causing him to cry out at the touch. If anyone had asked him his name right now, or even worse, called out an attack, he was 1000% certain he could not have stopped what they were doing. He wasn't even sure that he was a person anymore, just a part of the writhing mass of pleasure on that bed.

Still lower he worked, kissing his way down her belly, then slowly, delicately between her legs. The first touch of his tongue to that paradise was enough to make his balls ache, he was so close to coming. Somehow he managed to lick again, and then wind his long finger inside of her, probing for that sweet spot, feeling her clenching down on him with every slight motion. She grabbed his hair, pushing his face back towards where he was kneading. He had no intention of refusing. He heard her moans growing stronger as his tongue explored, mapping out a guide of all the places she enjoyed.

Was she screaming his name as he worked? The words sent a chill of pleasure down his spine as he moaned with her. Yes, this is what making love should be like. This was what he had been missing for all of eternity. Her. It was always her, only her. His wife-to-be. Goddess, he could ask her right now if only he could think for himself instead of being a slave to her moaning. He swore just one more sound and he would explode along with her.

He pulled himself up, back to her mouth, claiming it again as his own. Rocking his hips into her, he moaned when his cock met the wet area it begged to be allowed to explore. The kisses only made it harder to control himself. "Beloved, may I please- " he broke off to moan as she started stroking him. "Fuck Ase."

"Moan for me, my King."

He did just that, letting her tease him to heights he hadn't known existed until this very night. "Ase, I want to be inside of you. No, I need to be inside of you. Please, may I."

"Yes!" she groaned into his mouth as he kissed her.

Loki pulled her upright until she was sitting in his lap, before slowly working his way inside. "By the Norns, it is too much," he muttered, laying his head on her shoulder. "I will shatter if we do this, there will be no going back."

Holly pulled him closer to her, stroking his chest. "Then shatter. I am not going anywhere."

"Swear it to me," he demanded.

"Swear what my love?"

"Swear that if we do this, that you will still be here at morning light, and for every dawn after that. I cannot do this just to lose you," he begged. "I cannot give my heart again for it to be torn apart when you leave me."

"Loki, I am never leaving you until the day I die and given a choice, not even then. I love you. You are everything to me."

"As you are to me, my Ase. I could never leave you."

Loki eased his way inside of her, merging their bodies in the highest form of ecstasy as they moved together. Their moans could no doubt be heard at the other end of the cave system as they chased that sweetest of highs. Holly came first, screaming his name, wrapping herself around his body as tightly as she could, urging him to join her. Feeling that coolness inside of her as his precum started to leak. He couldn't last, she wouldn't allow it. Riding him harder, pushing him back on the mattress until she was on top. In control of everything. Taking him deeper, faster, harder, until she felt that coolness bloom inside of her as he screamed her name. The spread of his load taking her to a heavier, higher orgasm than she had ever experienced.

She collapsed onto the bed next to him, stroking his chest as he kissed her. Too exhausted from his first ever true love making session to even consider another round, he pulled her closer and kissed her. He used his magic to cover them in the rough sewn blankets. "Why did we never do that before?" he asked, as she settled her head on his chest.

"It would have saved a lot of the long, lonely nights in that castle," she answered, burying her face in his chest.

"Oh Ase, you stole my heart and my length."

She traced her name on the limp body part as they cuddled. "Mine now."

"I could never imagine it being anyone else's. I would cut it off and gift it to you before I allowed it to be anywhere near another person. You have my word."

"Good, I would cut it off myself if it even tried to."

"You have no need," he assured her, pulling her close. Sleep was pulling at him, not the usual black out drunk oblivion, but deep, real, exhausted, sleep. With Holly in his arms, he didn't even attempt to fight it off. He had everything he had ever desired right here.

Lucinda Greyhaven

Chapter Twenty-Five

… That Wasn't There Before.

Loki woke, panicking for a few moments until he felt the reassuring weight of his beloved sleeping on his chest. He smiled, playing with her hair as they lay there, feeling a level of contentment that he thought could never be his. She was beautiful, and kind, and passionate and well, she was everything. He couldn't even begin to understand why she was in love with him, but he would take whatever she would give for as long as she was willing to give it. He bent down to kiss her, nipping at her mouth.

Ase awoke, kissing him back just as passionately. "Hey."

"Morning beloved," he answered, a real smile on his face.

"Someone looks like he had a good night," she teased.

"I could have a much better morning now you are awake, if you are willing."

"My King is insatiable."

"I am a God."

"I am not."

"We can resolve that as soon as I can get to Idunn."

"Do you mean that you would make me a Goddess, just to make love to me for the rest of our lives?"

"I would make you a Goddess for a single smile," Loki admitted. "The sex is just an added bonus."

"All this time we wasted, when we could have been making love," Holly said sadly.

"Then let us make up for lost time," Loki suggested.

"As my King demands."

"Oh, your King has very many demands, he hopes his Queen can keep up."

• •

The next few days were spent in training, studying and preparing for the upcoming fight. Holly had much to learn and extraordinarily little time to do it in, throwing on heavier armour than she would be using while training, trying to strengthen her stamina. While still sneaking away for kisses with Loki whenever they had a spare private moment Thinking they were being ultra-sneaky, and that no one had noticed, they didn't realise how Frigg and Angroboda smiled at each other every time they excused themselves with a varied amount of ever-changing excuses. Thor held a conflicted look whenever he saw them together before shuffling away to train his army. Was that a look of regret on his face?

Angroboda disturbed the training. "Odin's troops collect on the plains. Thor, are you prepared to shadow the Midgardian through the battle for her protection?"

"I think my talents would be best served elsewhere. I am too strong, too powerful to be saddled babysitting the Witchling. Frigg should remain behind with her, keeping the baby out of danger," Thor objected.

"I need to be at the helm of the battle to speak with Odin, to try to force him to stand down from this battle. My baby is protected from harm, do not use my condition as an excuse to shirk your duties."

Loki pulled Thor to one side. "What is wrong? We spoke about this at great length. I need someone strong and skilled to protect my Ase. Someone who can hold their own in battle. You are Asgard's strongest warrior. This is where I need you. Do I not still hold your loyalty?"

Thor couldn't meet his friends' eyes. "My regrets, Lord Loki for questioning your battle plan. Of course, I will protect your Queen."

Loki grasped his shoulder. "Thank you, old friend."

Thor went back to sharpening his sword, looking vaguely upset.

Loki embraced Holly. "This is your night to shine, how do you feel?"

"Nervous."

"That never changes, however many battles you fight. If it does, remove yourself from the battlefield before you become a monster as wicked as your enemy," Frigg advised.

Angroboda grew impatient with all the talking. "Move out, we need to get ahead of these Asgardian troops."

"Wait!" Loki said. "I have something I want to say before we leave." He pulled the Midgardian closer to him. "Holly, you have been there for me through everything. You have turned my life around. You saved me when I was ready to give up and then you appeared like a bright guiding star, showing me that I had a reason to keep on living." He paused to gracefully get down on one knee, spreading his coat out behind him. "Ase, would you be so kind as to share the rest of your life with me?" He held out a ring, set with a green stone, surrounded by love runes.

Holly smiled back at her oldest friend, a mischievous grin on her face. "Before I answer that, just one question please."

"Anything, speak your wish and it is yours. Land? Gems? Jewels? Rich gowns? The best knives in the Nine Realms? It is yours, whatever you wish. What do you desire, my dearest love?"

"Do you still have that library?" she asked.

Loki stared at her for several seconds, they were moments from battle. Possibly both about to die, he was down on one knee, mostly sober with his heart on his sleeve, offering everything he was to the woman he loved, and she was trolling him. His wife to be, was teasing the God of Mischief. He had thought he couldn't love her any more than he already did, but he was wrong. Laughter bubbled up inside of him, spilling out until those around him thought he had lost his mind. "Oh, my Ase. I have taught you too well. The library is yours; it always was and as many books as your heart desires. One of every book in creation from every single realm."

Holly embraced him. She hugged him tightly, pulling him into a kiss.

"Ase, a little more vocal please. I am an old man, on my knees. Could you give me an answer before I die of old age? Which for me, would be quite a feat!"

"Yes, of course yes! How could I say anything else? I love you."

Loki allowed her to help drag him back onto his feet. He kissed her with the passion that was burning its way out of his chest. The part of him that had been yearning for someone who was truly his forever. When they pulled apart, she stroked her hair affectionately. "You just said yes for the books."

"No, dumb ass. I said yes for the drop dead gorgeous, sexy King who owns them." She leaned in closer. "And for the mind-blowing sex."

Loki smiled, one of his few genuine smiles. You could tell by the way it reached his eyes. "But the books help?"

"Yes Lokes, the books help. I love you, old man."

"I love you too Ase." Loki realised for the first time that they had an audience.

Frigg rolled her eyes. "Took you long enough."

"Can we start this battle now before the next Ragnarök comes? Or would you like the wedding, honeymoon and a few years of wedded bliss first?" Angroboda asked.

"Well, a wedding night would be nice. I am sure you can hold the line, while we just excuse ourselves," Loki agreed., "Just call us if things don't go to plan. Actually no, don't call us at all. We will be busy."

"Loki," Holly hissed, digging her elbow into his chest.

"No wedding night?" he asked.

"No wedding night until there is an actual wedding, and no risk of the realm being invaded," she replied.

"Damn it," Loki muttered. "How about…what do you Midgardians call it? Seven seconds of heaven?"

"Loki!" Holly exclaimed, looking embarrassed.

"What?" Loki asked. "I could die today, does that not at least gain me a little fun first?"

"Don't die and you can have all the fun you want after," she suggested.

"I will hold you to that."

"I'll hold you to something if you do not shut up," she warned.

"That sounds kinky, and quite interesting. Care to explain further?"

"Loki, I will cut off your manhood if you don't stop embarrassing me."

"Don't worry, we have all heard you two screaming every single night," Angroboda commented. "Do we expect an heir to the throne anytime soon?"

"I hate you," Holly said, burying her head in Loki's chest.

"No, you do not."

"No, I don't, but next time. Somewhere we can't be heard?"

"Perhaps I enjoyed the fact that we were?"

"Perhaps I will never have sex with you ever again."

"I will soundproof the castle chambers, do not concern yourself."

"You had better."

"Any other wild desires before I risk my life?"

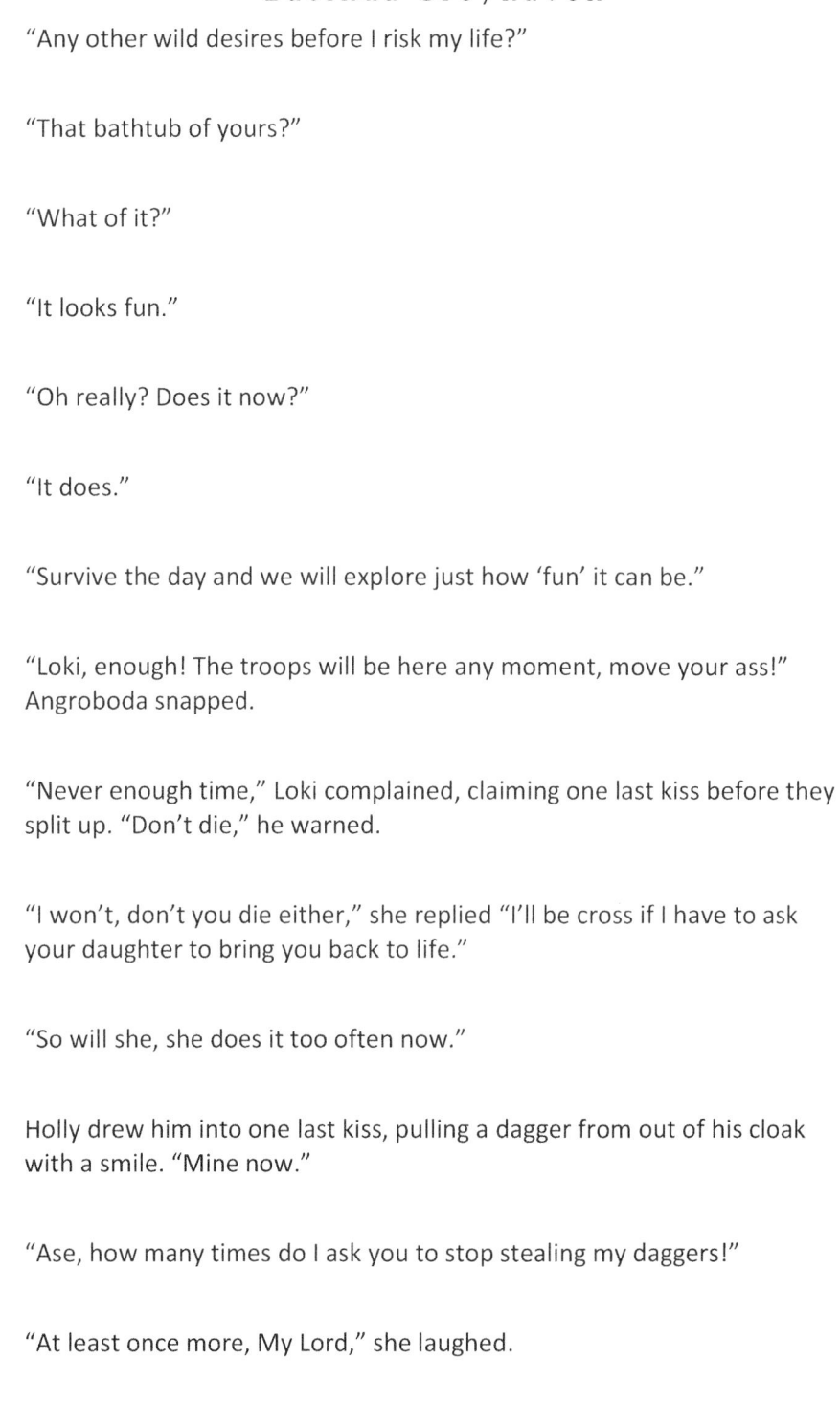

"That bathtub of yours?"

"What of it?"

"It looks fun."

"Oh really? Does it now?"

"It does."

"Survive the day and we will explore just how 'fun' it can be."

"Loki, enough! The troops will be here any moment, move your ass!" Angroboda snapped.

"Never enough time," Loki complained, claiming one last kiss before they split up. "Don't die," he warned.

"I won't, don't you die either," she replied "I'll be cross if I have to ask your daughter to bring you back to life."

"So will she, she does it too often now."

Holly drew him into one last kiss, pulling a dagger from out of his cloak with a smile. "Mine now."

"Ase, how many times do I ask you to stop stealing my daggers!"

"At least once more, My Lord," she laughed.

"You!" Loki chased after her half-heartedly. "Give me back that dagger."

"After the battle!"

Lucinda Greyhaven

Chapter Twenty-Six

Loki's Sacrifice

Holly called up the necromancy power that she had been hiding from for most of her life, letting the power swirl around her, feeling it rage like a storm around her. Collecting it until the power had grown large enough, she could summon what her husband to be needed. She closed her eyes, focusing on what was beneath the ice. The endless bones of the long since fallen warriors of his people. Pouring everything she had into the earth, she began raising up her army, pulling the long dead back towards the surface. The hue of magic around them as the frost giants came together was like something from a Ray Harryhausen movie. The leader looked at Holly for her instructions. "Destroy Odin and his warriors, follow Loki's every command," she ordered.

The reanimated Frost Giant tilted his skull to show his understanding before leading the army away. Holly pushed the magic she had through the earth as deep as she could feel, calling forth hundreds more warriors, watching as they joined the ranks of Loki's new army. She was drained, exhausted from her channelling. Where was Thor? He was meant to be here protecting her, dragging her out of the fight when her task was done. "Thor?" she shouted. She couldn't see him anywhere.

Holly staggered away, trying to dodge through the battlefield to somewhere she could rest. One of her shadows deflected a sword flying at her face, a small group of them huddled around her, building a shield wall to move her out of the battle unharmed. However, the problem with building a shield wall is it can clearly be seen in the battle as they moved through. A large moving target. No one attacked the convoy while they slowly crossed to safety. When they got to the side of the battlefield, it was a different story.

The beings left Holly at the mouth of the cave she had once shared with Loki, before they headed back to the battle. Holly drank the water that was waiting for her, shouting again for Thor. That was when Odin struck. She tried to defend herself, to crawl away, but her strength was spent. She was completely defenceless without Thor there.

The battle had never been about winning, Odin had just wanted to checkmate Loki by kidnapping his Queen. The Bifrost came crashing down, taking Odin, Holly and their army back to Asgard, stopping the battle mid strike. It was over.

■■■

Loki took his troops into battle, attacking Odin's army and cursing his name that he dared to attack Jotunheim once again. The frost giants were already near extinct from his past conquests. Loki had concerns they would lose today on their homeland, which would never be acceptable. Odin needed to be smacked back down, taught that regardless of his constant attempts to do so, the King and Queen of Jotunheim could not be driven apart. They were a united front, however much he wanted his shieldmaiden far from the battle and safe in his castle. His Ase would not stand for it, and she was needed on the fringes, raising the second army as they had planned. They would not last long without that added aid. Thor had better be there to get her away from the front when her task was done because if not, Thor would be spending an eternity under something far worse than a poisoned snake.

He glanced to where his wife to be stood, high on the mountain side, awaiting her cue to raise the dead. She looked every inch the Queen that he had made of her. A dirty thought crossed his mind about calling the whole thing off and taking her to his bed to show her just how majestic he could be. The problem since he admitted his feelings for her was keeping his hands off his wife to be for longer than a moment. He had not known anything like it before, he was acting like a hormonal teenager. When this was all over, he would take her on a honeymoon travelling the entire Nine Realms for a few centuries, in Midgardian terms. Coming back with his wife carrying his child would be his deepest desire. A child that could grow up free of Odin's influence. A child that would be safe.

He saw Holly smiling back to him, asking silently if it was time. He mouthed 'I love you' to her, seeing her smile broaden. His heart swelled, he was so painfully close to being perfectly, completely and eternally happy with her. The only thing he had ever wanted was love and acceptance. Ase did that and far more. He couldn't picture having a life without her.

Which of course meant he would soon have to.

Nothing that Loki dared to love ever stayed stable in his life. He could feel the dread washing over him as he gave her the nod to start work. He tried to push away the dark, insecure thoughts as he launched into the battle, knives and daggers flying everywhere as he attacked the Asgardian soldiers. War raged around him as he whirled, clashing blades with countless soldiers. Slicing awaylike he was in some murderous dance, like the King he was born to be. Loki kept going until there were no soldiers left. Until there was no one left on the battlefield apart from his own army.

Loki knew something was wrong, it stabbed him in the heart. Glancing around, he saw the Bifrost taking them away. He looked around at the tattered remains of the battle, there were some injured but Frigg would deal with those, the others only Hel would be able to bring comfort to. Their losses were nothing compared to what they could have been without Ase's help.

Ase, where was she? He couldn't feel her, she couldn't be dead. He wouldn't allow it. "Thor!" he bellowed, looking around more wildly. He made his way through the carnage to the cave. "Thor, Ase!" He found his way to the front of the cave but no one was there. The dread started to choke him. Something was wrong, very wrong. They had agreed to meet here and now he couldn't feel any of her magic. "Ase!" he shouted louder.

Thor appeared silently from inside of the cave, his eyes trained on the ground, not wanting to look at Loki. "I am sorry."

"Sorry for what? Where is my wife?" Loki demanded.

"Odin, he took Sif. I had no choice. Loki, Sif is with child. He threatened them both unless I aided him."

"Aided him with what? I am warning you!" Loki snapped, drawing a blade.

"Odin promised me he would let them go, if..." Thor trailed off.

"If you gave him my wife," Loki whispered.

Thor nodded. "I had no choice."

"You had every choice!" Loki snapped, slamming him against the cave wall by his throat. "You could have come to me! You could have told me, and we could have worked it out together without anyone being harmed!"

"And if it was her, could you have thought clearly?" Thor demanded. "I love my wife."

Loki brought the blade up, he wanted to kill the man standing there. Every instinct told him to destroy the man that had caused his wife to come to pain, but she would not have wanted him to do so. Holly hated violence for the sake of it. He slammed the Asgardian against the wall one last time before letting him go. "I need her, I can't live without her. She is my everything."

"And Sif is mine."

"Odin won't let either of them go easily."

"I am aware."

"I love her. I never thought I would be able to say those words again and mean them."

"Then let us save our women together," Thor suggested.

Loki looked at him in total disgust. "If it wasn't for you, Ase wouldn't need rescuing. Once I am done freeing her from Odin, watch your back 'King in Waiting of Asgard'. You will be the next monster I hunt. Now, be gone from my lands before I kill you where you stand for treason against my Queen."

"Loki please."

"I said leave!" Loki screamed. He turned his back on his blood brother as the Jotuns arrived, not caring what might happen to him. All he could think of was Ase, trapped alone with Odin and the unspeakable tortures that he would be putting her through. He had promised to keep his wife safe, to be by her side always and he had let her down. If she was to be tortured, they should at least be side by side suffering together.

"Ase, I will come for you. I love you," Loki vowed. "I will destroy the entire Nine Realms if that is what it takes to free you. I swear on my own existence you will be saved, even if it costs my life in return. You are the only person who matters anymore."

No more being Kingly, this would be an act of pure pain, revenge and anger to free Holly from the Oath Breaker.

Odin would die.

The End.

Jotunheims Queen

Lucinda Greyhaven
About the Author

Lucinda Greyhaven has been publishing since 2016 under her real name (Sarah Beth James) writing a mixture of contemporary romances and fantasy books. Moving to the new pen name in 2022 to branch off into mythology fantasy and a lot of hot Loki.

Book Two of the Frozen Hearts series will be out May 24th
Book Three of the Frozen Hearts series will be out winter 2023

For more information or for press contacts please follow:

Insta: authorlucindagreyhaven
Tiktok: @lucindagreyhaven
Twitter: @wickedwitchgal
Facebook Street Team: Books, Sass and Loki.

Acknowledgments

With thanks to everyone who helped me get this show back on the road after walking out my publishing deal.

I love you all so much.

See you all @ Enticed By Romance Booksigning

Newcastle April 27th 2024

Printed in Great Britain
by Amazon